THE COMPLETE CASES
OF DOC PIERCE

THE COMPLETE CASES OF
DOC PIERCE ™
VOLUME 1

RICHARD DERMODY

ILLUSTRATIONS BY
JOHN FLEMING GOULD
PETER KUHLHOFF

POPULAR PUBLICATIONS • 2022

TABLE OF CONTENTS

HELLO, SUCKER!

"I HAVE A PLEASANT SURPRISE FOR YOU," SPIELS THE SLICKER, "A FREE PAIR OF PREMIUM SPECTACLES FROM THE STATE AS PART OF OUR NEW PROGRAM." AND BEFORE THE GAPING APPLE-KNOCKER KNOWS IT, HE'S OUT A FIN, AND DOC PIERCE HITS THE STARTER AND IS WHIZZING DOWN THE ROAD.

T IS a cool morning and the woods and fields in northern Florida are a pleasant change from the sand and scrub pines around Miami. The doc's Chevvy is purring along and staying on the pace and the ham and eggs are taking hold so I feel pretty comfortable.

The doc stops cackling at a little story I tell him and begins to run his fingers around the edge of this high collar he is wearing. I figure a play is coming up as I notice him doing the same thing the night before whenever the dice go sideways on him. I do not have long to wait.

"I have a little confession to make to you, my young friend," he starts out. "I am afraid I will have to impose on you for a small financial accommodation until I can contact my banker. My glasses got fogged up last night after you left and I did not do so well in that game of chance or whatever it was."

I have been thinking this doc over and I am not surprised at this touch. When I met him in a gin-parlor in Jacksonville the night before I put him away as a solid citizen and the kind of people I like to associate with.

He is a big red-faced party with a swayback coat that splits over the quarters and a pair of these striped pants with no cuffs. He is also wearing a wide black hat and a pair of cheaters with a black tie-rope on them so when he

3

tells me that he is Doctor Pierce and is connected with the government of this state of Florida I am ready to believe him.

When I let on that I am a well-known figure around the turf and am even now on my way to New Orleans to take a bite out of the bookies, he tells me he is driving to Mobile and I am welcome to ride with him that far free of charge; so of course I am waiting for him in front of the hotel that morning.

As I said, though, I have been thinking him over and he does not add up quite so well in the daylight, although I cannot quite put a tag on him.

Anyhow, when I get dressed that morning I slip my roll into my shoe. I have twenty sawbucks and it makes quite a lump under my foot but I feel better with my dough where this state official or whatever he is can't make a play for it.

I try to stall him.

"I thought you said last night that you were a big somebody around Tallahassee."

"Well," he says, "I was in the employ of the taxpayers for several years but I am now in business for myself." He chuckles and pats me on the knee. "Surely a little harmless prevarication will not interfere with our budding friendship?"

I don't get it, but I tell him he is welcome to what few checkers I am holding, about three dollars and a half, all told.

The doc's face gets purple and for a minute I think he is going to bust right out of his collar.

"Look here, pony boy," he says. "Do you expect me to believe that you intended to make New Orleans on that kind of small change?"

"Have you got a small bill there,"
he says, "a two or a five?"

I tell him I plan to wire to some pals when we get to Mobile. I can see he doesn't swallow it but he stays pleasant.

"Well," he says. "This is an awkward situation but we will have to make the best of it. Maybe we can scrape up a few shekels from our country cousins as we go along."

He stops the car and opens up a suitcase and takes out a handful of dime-store spectacles and some long sheets of green paper that are printed up like insurance policies or court orders, with red and gold seals stuck all over them. He lays this stuff on the shelf back of the seat and we take off again. I can't make any sense out of this equipment but I don't ask any questions.

He drives along slowly for a couple of miles and then turns off the highway onto a gravel road leading back into the woods. It is a Sunday morning and there is not much traffic. The sun is shining and I am sitting back taking in the scenery when all of a sudden the doc steps on the brakes.

I LOOK around and find out we have stopped in front of a shacky old farmhouse. An appleknocker with a gray beard is leaning up against a rickety fence along the road.

The doc calls him over to the car.

"I am Doctor Pierce of the state department at Tallahassee," he says. "Who am I speaking to?"

The beaver says his name is Clayton.

"That's fine," says the doc, "you're just the man I want to see." He reaches back of the seat and holds out a pair of Woolworth binoculars. "Did you receive a pair of the premium spectacles, Mr. Clayton?"

Clayton takes the cheaters and mumbles he didn't hear tell about no spectacles.

"I have a pleasant surprise for you then," the doc tells him. "You have a free pair coming from the state as a part of our new program. I understand you are one of the largest landowners in these parts."

Clayton allows he's got a lease on three hun'erd acres.

"Splendid!" says the doc. "Of course you are familiar with the wonderful work we are doing over at Tallahassee. We are out to get the farmer the value of the high dollar. We're cutting out the middleman, the speculator, the profiteer and the gambler." He rattles it off like the auctioneer reading a yearling's pedigree at Saratoga.

He hauls out one of the long sheets of green paper. "This document will appoint you as our agent in your community. We'll send you literature every week right from the state capital and we want you to read it and speak for our program among your neighbors. Twice a year there will be a big meeting at Tallahassee with all your expenses paid. You'll be a guest of the state."

The doc stops to get his breath.

Clayton has hooked the spectacles over his ears and is standing there with his mouth open, drinking it in.

The doc turns and tips me a wink. "This is Doctor Allen," he says. "One of the brilliant younger members of my staff. I suppose you heard him lecture over at the court-house a few weeks ago?"

Clayton admits he heard tell of some doin's over yonder.

The doc holds the paper out the window. "Are the premium spectacles perfectly comfortable? Can you read the document?" He reaches out and settles the cheaters on Clayton's nose. "If the premium spectacles are not entirely comfortable I am sure Doctor Allen will be only too willing to make sure that you are properly fitted."

I still don't get the play but I know that I'm not having any. I tell the doc I can't help him.

He gives me a dirty look and snaps, "You're still pretty green, Doctor Allen. Maybe you'll wise up quick one of these days." He turns back to Clayton and chuckles. "We older people are apt to expect too much from the young folks, I sometimes think."

Clayton just goggles at him so the doc moves in for the payoff. He holds the green paper against the side of the car and produces a fountain pen.

"Just sign right here at the bottom of the document."

Clayton scratches some hen tracks on the paper and the doc snatches it away before he has a chance to read it.

"Now that you've signed the document and received the premium spectacles," he says, "I shall have to collect a few pennies for postage. As Doctor Allen often says, 'A two-cent stamp never hurt anybody.'"

CLAYTON GOES down into his clothes and comes up with a pouch about a foot long. He gets it unbuckled and plows up a couple of pennies.

The doc is jingling some silver in his hand.

"Have you got a small bill there, Mr. Clayton?" he says. "A two or a five? I have so much small change now that I am getting lopsided."

Clayton disappears into the poke again and comes to the surface with a fin. The doc grabs it and hands him a nickel.

"Thank you, my friend," he says very rapidly. "One hundred and ninety-seven stamps is exactly four dollars and ninety-five cents." He hits the starter and we are fifty yards down the road before Clayton gets his whiskers parted to start the beef.

The doc steps on the gas for a mile or two without doing any talking. I am thinking hard. I am beginning to get worried about those ten-spots in my shoe. From what I have seen of this doc he is apt to charm them right out into the open if I stay around him long enough. I am afraid to start a play myself because I realize this doc is two jumps ahead of me in any kind of going.

Finally he slows down and turns to me with a little smile on his face. "So you won't cooperate, pony boy?" He shakes his head. "Poor Mr. Clayton would be so much happier with his new premium spectacles if you had given him a little personal attention."

I tell him I don't want any part of this petty larceny he is carrying on and that he can unload me in the next town.

He just grins at me. "We don't get to any towns for quite a while," he says. "Maybe you'd like to get out here and wait for Mr. Clayton?"

I can't answer that one.

"Perhaps if you search yourself carefully you might find an odd twenty or so that you overlooked," he says. "Then we could get right back on the highway and head for Mobile."

I am willing to give a couple of twenties to make the pavement again but I know that if I admit I am holding anything at all I might as well hand him the whole roll so I dummy up.

We continue along these back roads nearly all the rest of the day. I have to hand it to this doc. He is the smoothest operator I ever saw. He hooks at least a dozen of these hayshakers for everything from aces to sawbucks. One victim even goes into his house and brings out a five-spot. Then he makes a second trip for a shotgun and gets one blast at us before we get out of range.

While we ride along between customers the doc tells me how this deal operates. He claims the law can't touch him because this document the suckers sign is a receipt for a pair of spectacles. The doc fills in the price according to the take.

He tells me that he gets his training around the carnival pitches back in the middle-west and he claims that John Harrison, the circus man, is the finest character that ever lived. "He was my boyhood hero," the doc says. "How he loved to hear a sucker squeal! The cry of the denuded Hoosier was music in his ears!"

THE ONLY foul ball the doc clips all day is a young stove-lid on his way home with one solitary checker in his poke. The doc coaxes the dollar out into the air and even gets a grip on one end of it but the smoke won't let go.

"Nossuh," he says. "I got to buy rations wid dis heah dolluh. If I go home widout it, my ole woman skin me."

The doc points out that this is state business and that he has signed the document. If he doesn't turn loose the doc will have to blow the whistle, he tells him.

"When de sheriff come aroun', I have de dolluh," the smoke claims.

"Nonsense," the doc says. "If we have to set the machinery of the law in motion to collect this paltry sum it will cost you twenty dollars and three months on the chain gang!"

The smoke is scared blue but he hangs on and finally the doc gives up.

It is late in the afternoon and we are still a long way from Pensacola and the ferry to Mobile when the doc decides to call it a day.

We come to a crossing and turn south past a group of buildings that the doc tells me is a turpentine camp. I notice a signboard that says the highway is ten miles ahead and I begin to relax.

About a mile down this road we come to a shack with a couple of gasoline pumps out in front. The doc pulls up and gets out a handful of currency. He arranges four ones in his hand with just the edges showing and says we will stop here for fuel.

A chunky filly about sixteen is in charge of the pumps and while she is loading the tank the doc climbs out and wanders into the shack. I follow along as I figure some kind of a play is coming up.

The doc gives the filly the exact change in silver for the gas and then peeks over her shoulder into the cash drawer. He still has the four ones in his left hand and suddenly I realize what he has in mind. I have heard of this caper but I have never seen it operate so naturally I am very much interested.

The doc is very smooth. "I see you have some ten-dollar bills in there, little girl," he says. "I wonder if you could spare me one of them in exchange for ten of these ones? I wish to send it to my dear old mother through the mail."

The filly hands the doc a sawbuck and he riffles the aces into the till, counting them aloud as they fall. I am watching closely because I know he has only four in his hand but I will swear that I see ten different pieces of lettuce drop into that drawer, one at a time.

The filly seems satisfied and we get back into the car. The doc tries the starter and nothing happens. He kicks it again and it groans but the motor is dead. I am getting nervous by this time and when a big husky walks out of the woods with a shotgun under his arm and comes up to the car I don't feel any better.

This party is about fifty years old with a square chin and the brightest blue eyes I ever look at. He is very polite and asks are we having trouble with the car.

THE DOC gets out and pulls up the hood and the big guy helps him take a gander at the insides. Finally they come up for air and the doc shakes his head. "I fear we will have to call in another opinion," he admits.

The big guy smiles and holds out his hand.

"My name is Turner," he says. "My eldest son is very handy around a car. He has gone down to the highway with the evening milk but he will be back soon."

The doc smiles. "I am Doctor Pierce," he says, "and this young man is Mr. Allen." He gives Turner a funny look and says, "Pardon me, Mr. Turner, but do you happen to come from Indiana?"

Turner nods. "Yes," he says. "I am a Hoosier. I was a minister of the gospel back in the corn belt but now I am a farmer and a very good one, too. I came down here for my health some years ago and I have never regretted it."

He turns to the filly, who has sidled up during the conversation. "This is my only daughter and the best business head in the family. She runs the filling station here while my six boys handle the farm work." He nods at the shotgun he is packing. "That gives me plenty of leisure for my favorite amusement, the hunting of small game."

I do not like being so close to this sixteen-year-old jail-bait and this artillery at the same time. It gives me the creeps. Also I am wondering about how long it will be before this career woman finds out the till is short six dollars.

The doc acts as though Turner has just paid off at thirty-to-one. He grabs his hand again and puts on a big smile. "This is indeed a pleasure," he says. "I spent the happiest years of my life in Fort Wayne."

Turner gets excited. "You must come over to the house and meet my wife and the rest of my little brood," he says. "My wife lived near Fort Wayne as a girl. She will be very happy to meet you."

I can think of plenty of things I had rather be doing but I follow the doc and Turner down a path through the woods. We come out on a clear space before the biggest log cabin I ever saw. It must be half a block long and has chimneys sticking up all over it. Turner says he has been building on it for ten years and I can believe it.

I notice an old mule going round and round on the end of a big log at one side of the house and I ask him if that is the way he works out his stock.

He tells me that it is a sugar mill and the mule is grinding cane. "We are a self-sufficient little unit here," he says. "We raise our vegetables and fruit and make our own butter and cheese. The woods abound with game and all my sons are fine shots."

I am liking this less and less as we go along and the idea of all these sharpshooters around the place does not make me feel any better.

WE MEET Turner's squaw and a few more of the tribe and after the doc and Mrs. Turner have finished putting in the boosts for good old Fort Wayne we go back to the gas pumps and stand around waiting for this mechanical wizard.

Finally an old flivver bounces up and a kid about twenty climbs out. The rest of the tribe are all huskies like the old man but this punk is about two axehandles across the shoulders and has mitts on him like Tony Galento. He tinkers with the doc's Chevvy for a while and tells us that the distributor has thrown a splint or something and we will have to put in a new one.

I give myself up when he says the earliest we can get one of these gadgets is the next morning as today is the Sabbath and the nearest garage, which is twenty miles away, is not operating.

The doc doesn't seem worried and inquires where we can get accommodations for the night. Of course Turner insists we bed down with him and after a little backing and filling the doc accepts.

Turner is so pleased I think he will bust a surcingle. He starts gabbing away to the doc about how profitable the filling station is right then. He says there is a boom in the turpentine business and all the boys at this camp up the road have jalopies and buy their gas from him. He says the take this weekend will run into a tidy sum.

I don't like this line of chatter as I figure the doc might get ideas in the middle of all this rural prosperity. The first chance I have I get him in a corner.

"Do you figure that gal isn't going to know who shorted her books for that six checkers?" I ask him.

He admits that the filly will probably start a beef if she finds out somebody made her for that score but he says he will think of some way to handle it. He looks at me with a kind of twinkle in his eye.

"You aren't thinking of ducking out on me, are you, pony boy?"

I tell him of course I will stick around.

"Well," he says, "I would not advise you to leave right at this time. I have a little plan that might work out unfavorably for you if you take a powder on me. I might suggest to Turner that I saw you lifting a few bills from the cash drawer just before you departed. I am certain the boys would have a lot of fun tracking you down."

I figure he probably has a little plan for me anyhow but I can't think of anything I can do about it.

We go back to the house with Turner and put on the chicken and black-eyed peas. The sharpshooters are all handy guys with a fork and the doc stows it away like a two-year-old but I am definitely off my feed.

After we pull out of the trough I mope over to the gas pumps and stand around talking to the filly. I am trying to think of some way of balancing the cash drawer before she finds out it's short.

SHE GOES out to wait on a customer and I get a brain wave. I slip off my shoe and get out my roll. I have the cash drawer open and am trying to sort out four ones from the pile, thinking I will replace them with one of my tens, when I hear a step on the gravel. Old Man Turner is coming through the doorway.

I don't have time to get my roll in my pocket so I drop it in the till and close the drawer. Even then I am not sure Turner has not seen the open till but he doesn't say anything.

I have my head down tying my shoelace when I hear the drawer slide open again. I nearly check out when I look up and see Turner standing there with my stack of tens in his mitt. He says something about how good business is but I am too punchy to understand it.

When I finally recover a little I hear him call out to the filly that he is taking all the large bills up to the house for safekeeping and that they will not balance the books until Monday when the rush is over.

I walk back to the house with Turner as I want to keep as close to my dough as possible and also I do not want him to think I am making a play for his daughter. I have enough troubles as it is.

For a minute I think of putting the slug on him while we are walking through the woods but I take a look at him and realize I am not built for the job.

I don't let the doc in on this news about the books not being checked until Monday. Let him worry. I am doing plenty of it. My roll is gone and I can't think of any way of getting it back without a lot of awkward explanations. And I figure the doc can out-explain me in any company.

Turner parks us in a big bedroom with a fireplace in the corner. The bunks are comfortable although these corn-shuck mattresses wake you up every time you turn over. I wake up once and see the doc rustling around in my keester in the moonlight. I figure he is making sure I have not got a few bucks stached away in it. I only wish I have. I would gladly split with him.

In the morning Turner's wife comes in with a pitcher of hot water and lights up the fireplace. I am standing around watching the doc scrape his face with an old-style razor like the smokes up in Harlem use for social gatherings and I notice this collar of his laying on the bureau.

I pick it up and look it over. It is made out of some thick material and I ask him what it is. He says it is cloth with rubber in it and very handy as you do not have to send it to the Chinaman. You just mop the dust off it with a damp rag yourself. He claims one of them will last for years and is very economical. I notice the doc has got quite a neck on him as this choker is size seventeen.

Turner walks in and wishes us a good morning. He takes the doc's collar away from me and chuckles. "I never see one of these collars in this country," he says. "I always wear them myself and brought a supply with me when I came to this state. I have several of them left and will probably be buried in one of them as I do not have much occasion to dress up nowadays."

THE DOC mumbles something through the lather and Turner stands there bending this collar back and forth. All of a sudden it flips out of his hand and lands plop in the fireplace which is putting out a lot of heat by this time. Before any of us can get to it, the collar is long gone.

The doc jumps about two feet into the air and nearly guzzles himself with the razor. Turner is very much upset and rushes out of the room saying he will replace it immediately with one of his.

The doc is in a state of mind. He lets out a stream of the worst language I ever hear and for a minute I think he is going to pop a blood vessel. This red face of his gets as green as the infield at Belmont and he has trouble getting the breath for all he wants to say.

I have trouble figuring why a cool hand like the doc should get in such a heat about a collar, even a rubber one, but I realize that most guys have a kink in them somewhere and maybe this haberdashery is the doc's private angle.

Turner comes in with another collar and the doc cools out and thanks him very politely for the loan. He promises to send it back by parcel post but Turner insists he keep it as a little memento of his visit.

The mechanical red-hot shows up at breakfast and says the doc's Chevvy is ready to roll. The doc wants to pay off but Turner slips the kid the nod and he refuses to tell the doc how much he paid for the gadget. Turner says the doc must allow him to show some real southern hospitality to an old neighbor from Indiana.

After a lot of bowing and scraping on both sides we take off in the Chevvy again. Although I am still sweating over losing my two C's I am pleased to be getting out of this area and back onto pavement. I can't help wondering how Turner and the jail-bait are going to get the books balanced with all that extra sugar in the kick.

The doc is silent and keeps running his finger around his collar the way he does when the pressure is on. I am curious about this uproar he raised when his collar goes up in smoke and I poke him a little to see how he will react. I can afford to jig him now that I have no bankroll to protect.

"It was very handy," I tell him, "that this Turner has a collar like the kind you are so attached to. 'Collar-attached Pierce,' that's you, doc," I tell him.

He grunts and gives me a sour look.

I grin back at him. "I don't suppose you could slicker these spectacle customers of yours in a regular collar," I tell him.

The doc stays dummied up so I take another fly at him. "Anyhow, you have lots room to move in. This Turner is a couple of sizes bigger than you are around the tonsils."

"Of course," the doc says, very snappy. "This Turner has a neck like one of his mules. This thing is at least size seventeen. I wear a sixteen," he says.

"Your zipper is loose, doc," I tell him. "That collar on the bureau this morning was a size seventeen. I noticed it special because very few people are that big around the neck."

THE DOC stops the car and takes me by the arm. His hand is shaking. "Are you absolutely sure that collar was a size seventeen?" He speaks very low and he is dead serious.

I tell him of course I am sure.

He slumps for a minute and then sits up and begins to produce the bad language from the beginning again. I listen respectfully for a while and then I ask him what is the score.

He just looks at me for a minute. "This Turner is no preacher," he says, very deliberate. "In fact he is a very sinister character. He filched my collar last night while I was a guest in his home and tore it open and extracted the eight hundred dollars I had sewn up in it and substituted one of those he had brought from Indiana."

I ask if it is a habit for him to keep his dough in his collar and he tells me it is a favorite hiding place among the pitchmen around the carnivals in the middle west.

He grabs me again. "That's it!" he hollers. "That's what made me think I had seen him before. That's why I asked him if he was from Indiana. I thought it was his speech at first but now I am sure. That one-thing-and-the-other was no preacher. He was a con man and a hypo artist. That's how he knew where to look for my roll. He pegged me the minute he saw me!"

I feel pretty sick. "That old joker must have seen me put that dough in the till," I blurt out.

The doc stares at me. "Don't tell me he made you for a score, too, pony boy?"

I need sympathy so I tell him about my idea of slipping a ten in the drawer and taking four out so the books will square up and how Turner walked in and I have to drop the whole two C's in the till.

The doc feels better already. He cackles and hollers until I think he will fall out of the car.

"Maybe that will teach you not to hold out on your superiors," he tells me.

Finally he quiets down. "Well," he says, "I doubt if we will obtain justice by going back and arguing with Turner or whoever he is. I have a feeling we would wind up full of buckshot. I guess we will just have to absorb our losses."

He starts up the car again and we move on down the road. We get a couple of miles along and we meet a haywagon with an old party in white whiskers in charge.

The doc slaps on the brakes and leans out the window.

"I am Doctor Pierce from the state department at Talla-hassee."

I reach back and open the suitcase. I am only too glad to be Doctor Allen and lend a hand with the premium spectacles.

THE DOCTOR'S BAG

THE DOC GOES INTO HIS SPIEL.
"I HAVE NEVER REGRETTED,"
HE INFORMS THE LOCAL APPLE-
KNOCKERS, "GIVING UP MY
PRACTICE TO DEVOTE MYSELF
TO SERVING MANKIND." AND I
LET OUT A CACKLE THAT NEARLY
SPOILS THE PITCH. THE DOC HAS
NEVER PRACTICED AT ANYTHING
IN HIS LIFE—HE HAS BEEN
PLAYING FOR KEEPS SINCE HE IS
OLD ENOUGH TO SPOT AN ANGLE.

WE LAND in this Millwheel late in the afternoon and the doc insists we hike right over to the local paper and get the bait planted. I watch over his shoulder while he is writing the ad.

> Have twenty thousand dollars to invest. Prefer new industry or established firm wishing to expand.

It looks tasty, at that, and I notice the bald-headed little guy behind the counter gives it a good going-over when the doc slips it to him.

The doc glances at the sign on the window and sticks his hand across the counter. "Mr. Vernon Billgate?"

The little guy nods and pumps the doc's mitt. "Editor and publisher of the *Millwheel Mirror*," he says, very snappy. "The fastest growing daily in western Georgia!" I can hear a lot of rattling and banging going on in the back room so I figure the local lowdown is even now sizzling off the presses.

The doc tilts his wide black skimmer off his forehead and parts his swayback coat so Billgate can get a load of his white vest. He has a pleased grin on his big red face so I know he is fitting this editor and publisher into the schedule. He hauls out a shiny alligator case and drops a card on the counter.

Billgate slides his fingers over the card, his eyes bug open and he squares up his cheaters and takes a good gander at it. I can see now why the doc insists on spending dough for first-cabin literature.

The doc makes another trip into his clothes and comes up with his wallet but Billgate shakes his head. "There will be no charge for this ad, Doctor Pierce," he says. "As a director of the Millwheel Chamber of Commerce I am only too glad to welcome new capital to the community." He takes another peek at the card. "I see you are president of the United Appliance Corporation, Warmingdale, Indiana." He pushes his hand across the counter again. "I am from the old Hoosier State myself!"

I don't feel so good. The last time we run up against a guy from the old Hoosier State he clips us for every dime we have. The doc clamps onto Billgate's mitt and spreads his smile a couple more inches.

"This is indeed splendid," he says. "I suppose you are familiar with our little corner of the grand old commonwealth?"

Billgate shakes his head and says he never got around to that section of the fatherland. The doc lets his breath out and I can feel him relax. He transfers Billgate's mitt to my custody.

"This is Mr. Allen," he tells him. "Mr. Allen is an auditor and has charge of our accounting department."

I stiffen up and try to look like I am in charge of an accounting department. I wish now I had let the doc talk me into wearing a pair of these horn-rimmed cheaters. I don't have to worry though, I am just a detail to Billgate. He pumps my hand, lets me have a peek at the mailorder crockery he is hiding in his mouth and turns back to the doc. He seems quite taken with the doc.

I figure it is time to go.

"I presume you are at the Jefferson House," he says. "I am a resident there myself and I would be honored if you will dine with me tonight."

The doc says he will be delighted to put on the feed-bag with him and for a minute I think Billgate is going to crawl right over the counter and kiss him. He makes another grab at the doc's mitt but the doc sidesteps and heads for the outside. As we start down the main stem I look back. Billgate is still hanging over the counter goggling at us. The doc grins at me.

"I wonder if the *Millwheel Mirror* could use a little fresh dough?" he says.

WE HAVE the best accommodations at this Jefferson House, a three-room spread they call the Parlor Suite. The bunks are good but the place is jammed with the worst bunch of stuffed birds and other junk I ever see outside of a South Street hock shop. The doc is quite pleased with the layout, though, and when Billgate checks with us before dinner the doc invites him to come in and admire our quarters.

I am all sharpened up in a white flannel number I invest in when a Black Tony filly bobs up at sixty-to-one the week before in New Orleans, and the doc has moved into his best pair of striped pants. He breaks out a jug of bourbon and we are ready to go to work.

Billgate turns out to be quite handy with the bourbon and by the time we are ready to put on the feed-bag he is sweating gently and speaking freely.

"It is some time since I have the pleasure of meeting up with fellow Hoosiers," he says. "The people here are slow to take up with newcomers and I have often been lonely during the three years since I invest my life savings in the *Millwheel Mirror.*"

I am not too strong for this crack about fellow Hoosiers as I am Brooklyn born and bred, but I let it ride as I do not want to embarrass the doc.

"Yes," Billgate says, "I have often been lonely, although I have hopes that this condition may soon be alleviated."

The doc leans forward and I can see he smells an angle.

"I gather that you have a romantic interest in some female in the locality?" he says.

Billgate takes another wallop at the bourbon and nods his bald head. "Yes," he says. "A lady named Mrs. Belinda Clotts, a charming person with a fine head for business. In fact," he tells us, "she owns and operates the largest box-factory in these parts."

"That is most interesting," the doc says. "I have been a close observer of recent industrial trends and I feel that the development of factories in this region is a splendid thing for the future of the nation. That is why I suggested this section to my board of directors as a possible field of investment for our surplus funds. I should like to meet Mrs. Clotts."

Billgate snatches the telephone. "Perhaps we can persuade her to dine with us this evening," he says. While he is talking to Mrs. Belinda Clotts the doc moves over to me and drops his voice.

"Five will get you fifteen," he says, "that this female is in the market for fresh dough, and five will get you twenty that Billgate talks me out of running that advertisement. Billgate is a greedy little man," he says, "and wishes to keep this touch all to himself!"

I just grin at him. "You know that you are strictly six-to-five in my book on any proposition, Doc. I will play the line on this one and skip the side-bets."

MRS. BELINDA CLOTTS is maybe forty and not a bad-looking old pelter at that. When she sits down at the table I notice she is legged up good and from the way she is built up around the chest I figure her wind is O.K., too.

I notice the doc inspects her points very carefully and for a minute I think he is going to ask Billgate to trot her up and down the lobby so he can see how she moves, but then I realize he is probably only trying to figure out which sock she carries her roll in.

She has a soft voice like a lot of dames in those parts and she doesn't have much to say so I begin to think she may not be as big a nuisance as I expect. I like my deals and my dames straight and I know many smart operators who jinx themselves by mixing them up, but as long as this dame is in this deal I am glad she is not gabby about it.

Nobody is very gabby for quite a while after we gather around the trough. This Jefferson House is one of these hayshaker outfits where they line up the rations in the middle of the table and no holds barred. I always eat like a two-year-old and the doc is a good doer himself but when he sees the plaster Billgate is putting away he sends for a bottle of wine as he does not want Billgate to lose the edge he puts on him with the bourbon.

Billgate finally gets the wrinkles out and slows down to let his tools cool off.

"Doctor Pierce is the head of a large corporation in my old home state, my dear," he tells the dame. "He is looking for opportunities for investment in this part of the country and I think we should demonstrate the true Georgia hospitality and assist him in every way."

The dame gives the doc a big white smile and says she is happy to oblige. I settle down to enjoy myself. I always like to watch the doc making a pitch and as this is the first time I have helped out on this kind of a caper I am naturally paying very close attention.

The doc fills the glasses all around with vino and sets to work.

"Yes," he says, "the United Appliance Corporation has flourished like the green bay tree of Holy Writ during the past few years. We manufacture artificial aids for the physically handicapped and the recent shocking increase in highway accidents has contributed to our prosperity in no small measure."

Billgate washes the dust out of his throat with a slosh of vino and says what a sad thing it is, all those cripples, and what a splendid work the doc is engaged in, patching them up.

I have to let out a cackle when I hear this as I know that the United Appliance Corporation is nothing but an old one-legged uncle of the doc's who has a woodworking shop in his barn out in Warmingdale, Indiana, where he turns out new pegs for himself and a few of the neighbors.

The doc glares at me and I cover up by flagging the stove-lid who is waiting on us and directing him to bring another jug as I know the doc does not want Billgate to run out of fuel.

Billgate and the dame do not pay any attention to my break. They are hanging on the doc's words as though they expect him to whip out a check-book any minute. Billgate is letting his chin hang down a little and I can see a gap where his upper section of crockery has loosened up. I don't mention it to him. After the punishment he has been giving the provisions I figure his choppers are entitled to relax.

The doc takes aim at the dame. "I feel that our company is performing a necessary service and I have never regretted the step I took when I gave up practicing to devote all my time to its affairs."

I NEARLY let out another cackle. The doc has never done any practicing at anything in his life. He has been playing for keeps since he is old enough to spot an angle.

The dame likes it. "I can understand that," she says. "I have enjoyed working out the problems involved in the operation of the little business I have managed since Mr. Clotts passed on. It is a small business now," she tells him, "but we own plenty of pine trees out of which we make boxes and if we can expand our plant a little I am sure we can compete with the larger concerns up north."

Billgate wags his chin like he wants to get in on the play but his choppers stick and he just lets out a big hiss. Before he gets them snapped back into place the doc is on his feet and I realize he is winding up the pitch.

"We must have a long talk soon about the future of your enterprise, Mrs. Clotts," he says. He bows at Billgate. "I hope you will excuse us for ending this very pleasant evening but we have had a tiring day and must be fresh tomorrow."

I start to cackle the minute we are safe in the Parlor Suite. The doc gives me a dirty glare.

"Listen, pony boy," he says. "I cut you in on this caper because I figure you are smart enough to hold still at the right time. That jackass bray you let out tonight might have queered this whole operation."

I tell him I am sorry but every time I think of this peg-leg relative and his shop I have to laugh. The doc grins a little himself.

"I must confess I get a certain amount of amusement out of it myself, even after all the years I have been using Uncle Jabez as a front. Uncle Jabez is a dear old man," he tells me, "and it would break his heart if he knew the real reason I had him incorporated many years ago. In fact," he says, "Uncle Jabez would be even more upset if he knew what might happen to him if anybody traced certain matters all the way back to Warmingdale."

I stare at him. "Do you mean to say Uncle Jabez will take the rap if somebody blows the whistle on us in this deal?" I never realize before what a really tough cookie this doc is.

The doc pats me on the shoulder. "Don't strain yourself listening for that whistle," he says. "If there is one thing in this world a sucker hates worse than a trimming, it is for the other suckers to know that he has been trimmed!" He opens his suitcase and takes out a couple of books. "Let's get to work. I want to give you a quick once-over on ledgers tonight. I have a feeling you may be in action before long."

I have been working out on form-sheets around the tracks for years and I am not too dumb at figures but the doc has been pumping this auditor and accountant routine into me pretty fast for the past week.

"O.K.," I tell him, "but load me light, I may break down in the stretch run if you weight me too heavy!"

THE NEXT morning Billgate is laying for us at breakfast and while we are putting on the ham-and-eggs and he outlines his plans for our day.

"Millwheel still supports one of those ancient institutions known as a livery stable," he says, "and I often rent one of their equipages and drive through the surrounding countryside. I find it very restful."

"I hope you invite me to accompany you while I am here," the doc says. "It will take me back to the days when I was a struggling medical student and sold classical literature from farm to farm to earn my tuition."

Billgate looks like he has just been handed a ripe peach. "As it happens," he says, "I had intended to rent a rig this very morning as I have a few calls to make. I should be pleased to have you accompany me."

"Splendid!" the doc says. "It will help to pass the time until I receive a few answers to my advertisement."

Billgate starts pushing his coffee cup around in little circles. "About that ad of yours," he says. "I have been giving it some thought and I think you might be wiser to carry on a quiet investigation of various industries in the vicinity."

He snickers a little. "Most of them are in need of funds and some of them might be inclined to paint a rosier picture than the facts justify."

The doc helps him along. "You mean that some unscrupulous person might take advantage of the fact that I am a stranger?"

Billgate nods, very solemn. "I am sorry to say that there are a few wolves among the sheep, even in this quiet pasture."

I know the doc will spot any wolf in the country a couple of bites but he looks solemn, too. "Perhaps you are right," he says. "Perhaps you had better hold that advertisement for a few days, at least."

Billgate hops up from the table. He is so tickled that he forgets all about a slab of ham the size of a barn door he has been working on. "I will have them harness Henrietta right away," he says. "Henrietta is the snappiest horse they have. I am sure you will like her." He hustles to the door and then stops and looks back. "I will even let you drive Henrietta," he promises.

The doc shakes his head and grins at me. "This Billgate is a busy little man," he says. "I wonder what he and the widow found to talk about last night after we left?"

"I didn't listen to them," I tell him, "but five will pay you fifty that they have plans to soak up all of that twenty G's they think you are holding."

The doc nods. "I fear they sliced me very thin, at that!" He glances out the window. "I see Ben-Hur and the chariot are waiting. You had better hole up in the Parlor Suite while we are gone," he says. "Apply yourself to your lessons and do not let any of these wolves Billgate tells about get at you."

I go out to see the doc get Henrietta away from the barrier as I figure there may be a laugh in it.

Henrietta is a big rangy chestnut with a lot of daylight under her and outside of having feet like frying-pans and a head the size of a beer-keg, she is not badly put together.

The doc gathers up the reins like an old hand, lets off a couple of loud clucks and Henrietta bowls away down the pike with her tail stuck up like a hackney. The doc will make two of Billgate and leave enough over for a fair-sized midget so the buggy is all sagged down on the off side. Every time they go over a bump Billgate slides down the seat and brings up in the doc's lap, so I get my laugh, at that.

I spend the morning working out on the auditing and accounting and after lunch I take a mope around the town. This Millwheel is a fair-sized burg but I don't find any action. The dames are all wrinkled up and hiding under sunbonnets or they have pappies and big brothers with them and a guy in a cigar store nearly calls a cop when I ask him for a racing form, so I finally go back to the Parlor Suite and snap paper clips at the stuffed birds.

THE DOC comes in about five o'clock and I can see he has had a good day. He opens his vest so this haybelly he hides under it can slide into his lap and pours himself a jolt of bourbon. I wait until he cools out a little and then, after a few moments, inquire if Henrietta lasts out the distance.

"Henrietta had an easy day," he tells me. "By a rare stroke of good fortune we happened to take a road that passes right by this box factory owned by Mrs. Belinda Clotts." He chuckles. "Surprisingly enough, Mrs. Clotts, or Belinda as she has asked me to call her, happened to be right on the spot."

"Well," I tell him. "It looks like Billgate is spoiling for action. When do I start my play?"

The doc frowns and I can see he is thinking hard. "Of course I spent the whole day casing the joint with them and I have laid all the necessary groundwork. The only hitch is that Belinda is a little short of ready cash and we may have to wait until she collects a few outstanding accounts."

"How much of a score will they hold still for?"

The doc chuckles again. "Billgate confided to me that if he can get his hooks on ten grand he can run all the other papers in the county bow-legged and show a handsome profit. I assured him that I would recommend the investment to my board of directors provided that your audit of his books justified the claims he has been dinning in my ears all day. Of course I tell him that he will have to stand the expense of your fee, but he doesn't bat an eye at that. I think he will cash out for about three hundred dollars."

"How about the haybag?" I ask him. "Can she get by on the other ten grand?"

The doc scowls. "I wish you would clean up your vocabulary," he tells me. "Belinda is no bag, she is a charming and cultured woman and much too good for the likes of this Billgate!"

I don't like this at all. "Listen Doc," I tell him. "No matter what she asks you to call her, she is just a second-hand old bag in my book, and anybody with any sense will tell you the same thing. Let us get this play rolling and wind it up fast. If we stick around too long this haybag will put the arm on you."

The doc pays no attention. "I have indicated to Belinda that twenty thousand is a small portion of the resources of my company. She can use fifty G's very comfortably, she tells me. We are to dine together tonight and I will have her lined up in no time at all."

"Well," I tell him, "if she can use fifty thousand I will have to charge her at least a grand for the audit. Or maybe you will make her a special rate because she lets you call her Belinda!"

The doc scowls again. "Belinda will be the real touch," he says. "Her fee will amount to twelve hundred dollars which, with the three we snag from Billgate, will give us a grand total of fifteen hundred we will carry away with us!"

I feel better. "O.K.," I tell him, "you handle the dame, but keep out of dark corners."

I am asleep when the doc rolls in that night and he doesn't have much to say the next morning. He ducks Billgate and heads off into the country driving Henrietta so I figure he is going to put in some more work on Belinda.

That evening he is all steamed up when he gets into the Parlor Suite. "Billgate is all set," he tells me. "You can start working his books over in the morning. I figure you better mess around with him for about three days and by that time Belinda will be rounded up and ready for picking." He peels off his pants and starts for the bathtub. "I am dining with her again tonight," he says.

NOW THAT I am up against the gun I feel nervous. "Maybe you better stick around the *Mirror* office tomorrow in case I get jammed up."

The doc shakes his head. "You won't have any trouble," he assures me. "Just tell the bookkeeper to hand you the ledgers and stay away from you. Scribble a bunch of figures on a lot of small pieces of paper and mess them up on the desk. I have put you away with Billgate as a very temperamental guy when you are working so if anybody bothers you, let out a couple of screams and walk out. I can always smooth you over afterward."

I go like a breeze in the *Millwheel Mirror* office the next morning and I am feeling pretty chipper when I mope over to the hotel for lunch. I am standing around the lobby waiting for the bell when I spot the doc pussyfooting down the stairs. He gets a peculiar look on his red face when he sees me and at first I figure he is up to some dodge he doesn't want me to know about. Then I figure it is some kind of a curve he is pitching to this Belinda and I gave up trying to work out those angles many years ago.

I give the rations a workout as usual but the doc seems nervous and is off his feed for the first time since I know him. He doesn't even grin when I tell him I hope Billgate and his bookkeeper are trying to unscramble the mess of papers I have been cluttering up with figures all morning. I am sure then that he is carrying that old torch so I prod him a little.

"You ought to give up these capers and settle down, Doc," I tell him. "You are getting pretty long in the tooth and you don't get the laughs you used to. I really think you ought to get married, Doc." He just grunts so I pour a little more on his sore back. "Maybe you could marry up with this Clotts haybag and be a big somebody around that box factory. You could tell her that Uncle Jabez lammed out with all the assets of the corporation and you need a home!"

The doc just scowls at me and walks out. A few minutes later I see him go by the window with Henrietta in full stride. As I watch, he pops her a couple with the whip and I know I have scored on him. It hands me a laugh and maybe it is a good thing, at that. I don't get much chance to laugh during the rest of that day.

IT IS getting along toward sundown and I have quite a raft of papers all scrawled up with figures when Billgate comes into the office. I scowl at him and let on I am too busy to be disturbed.

He walks over to the desk and stands staring at me and for the first time I notice that he has very hard black eyes. Maybe it is because he is not wearing his cheaters.

"Get your coat on, wise guy!" he tells me. "You are going for a little ride!" He grabs my papers off the desk, wads them up and slams them on the floor. "This is the end of the line, wise guy!" he says.

I slip my coat on and get set to put the slug on him when I notice that he is pretty wide across the shoulders, at that, and he has a lot of ink smudged on his hands. I figure I might get my new white flannels dirty if I tangle with him so I step back and hold still.

Billgate laughs, and it is a very nasty laugh. "The sheriff is on his way to pick you up," he says. "And while you and that medicine-show phoney you travel with are spending the next few years in stir you can tell him that I held down the police beat for the *Journal* in New York for ten years and I can spot a con man as far as I can smell one. And do you chumps smell!"

I figure it is time to go. Billgate is between me and the door but the window is open. I spin a chair at Billgate and do a Brodie out the window. He follows and grabs me by the shoulder as I land but I shake loose and take out across the fields at a lively clip.

I do a couple of miles at a good smart canter and by the time I reach the road I am all in. I hole up in the brush until I hear Henrietta clopping along and then I jump out and flag her down.

Henrietta is startled and sticks her toes in very sudden. The doc jolts forward off the seat and embraces the dashboard. If this buggy had a windshield he would have stuck his head clean through it. As it is, Henrietta fetches him a couple of swipes across the face with her tail before he gets sorted out.

When he hears my story he looks sick. "A police reporter!" he says. "No wonder he wouldn't run that advertisement!"

HE SITS very still for a minute and I can see he is thinking hard. Finally he tells me to get into the buggy and he starts to turn Henrietta around. Henrietta gets very mad at this idea because she has been figuring she was on her way to the barn and a good hot mash. She puts up a stiff argument but the doc has no patience with her and belts her a couple with the big end of the buggy whip so after awhile she agrees to go back down the road away from Millwheel and this hot mash.

I suggest to the doc that maybe we better abandon Henrietta and take to the fields as I figure this local law will have wheels under him and is apt to catch up with us. Especially as Henrietta is not showing much speed.

The doc snorts. "I am comfortable right where I am," he says. "And this operation has been strictly within the law. Although," he says, "I would not care to face a jury in this county. I have found these crackers entertain some very primitive ideas and are only too prone to act without due regard for legal technicalities."

"Let's sneak back tonight and prowl that hotel for our luggage anyhow," I suggest. "The only five hundred dollars I have in the world is back there in the trick bottom of my keester."

The doc shakes his head. "Your five bills are not in your suitcase," he tells me. "Belinda needed a thousand to meet her payroll and I only had five hundred in my own pants pocket so I borrowed your roll this noon to make up the difference. I figured it was a good move—it would put me away with her as a solid man."

It is my turn to look sick. Now I realize why he was so jittery at lunch. "You are a solid man, at that," I tell him. "In fact we are a pair of solid men. Solid in the skull! A Hoosier and a haybag! And we were suckers enough to tackle a parlay like that!"

The doc nods. "We overmatched ourselves again," he says. "And I have to tender you an apology for scorching your remarks about Mrs. Clotts. Mrs. Clotts is not only a bag, she is a baggage!"

I watch Henrietta's stern doing a slow kootch between the shafts. "Anyhow, we don't walk out of town this time," I tell him. "Henrietta is still up and doing. She is one dame that has not been a jinx to us. I am glad we know Henrietta," I say, "because I am still recovering from that cross-country I put on a while back."

When I say this the doc lets out a screech as though somebody jabs him with a pitchfork. He hops out of the buggy and yanks me after him. I think he is off his rocker until I sort out what he is yelling. "They lynch guys that steal horses in these parts!" he hollers.

I help him turn Henrietta around again. It is no trick this time as she is willing to co-operate. The doc ties the reins around the whipstock and the last we see of Henrietta she is heading for the hot mash.

It is getting dark and as we hoof it along the road I am thinking about those soft bunks in the Parlor Suite and the row of hot platters they place in the middle of the table at the Jefferson House. I am thinking how pleasant it will be if Billgate and Mrs. Belinda Clotts choke on the next piece of fried chicken they work on, even if I am not there to see it.

After a mile or so I pull up and wait for the doc, who is not legged up for this kind of going. He is also puffing like a switch engine and I tell him I will have to start wetting his hay as he sounds like he might be getting a touch of heaves.

He parks his big quarters on a culvert and sits looking up at me. "What happened to your coat?" he asks me.

I pull off the white flannel and look at it. There are two black smudges down the middle of the back. I remember, then.

"That guy Billgate is just plain ornery," I tell him. "He had no intention of holding me when he grabbed me after I jumped out the window. He just wanted to mess up my coat with his inky mitts!"

The doc nods. "Of course he didn't want to hold you! Why should he? He shakes his head. "We have just financed a dandy honeymoon for that rascal and that old bag of his, Belinda!

THE DOCTOR OPERATES

"LISTEN CAREFULLY, PONY BOY," SAYS THE DOC, REACHING FOR THE BOURBON, "I HAVE A LITTLE OPERATION IN MIND TO CURE OUR AILING FINANCES... NOW ALL YOU HAVE TO DO IS PICK THE LOSING NAGS AND I WILL MAKE THEM PAY OFF."

I **AM** all beat out when I come into the room, what with dodging Pinkertons all afternoon and trying to convince the chumps that I am not personally responsible when these good things I tell them about do not always pay off.

The Doc is sitting in his underwear with his striped pants hanging by the cuffs from the top drawer of the wardrobe and his sway-back coat and white vest draped over a chair. He is dosing himself out of a bottle of bourbon and he looks cool and relaxed.

"How about you getting off that lard once in a while and hustling a few checkers?" I ask him.

The Doc takes a gulp of the bourbon and grins. He taps the side of his white-thatched head. "Up here is where I do my hustling, pony boy," he tells me. "I am packing too much weight for this leg work."

"Well," I tell him, "you had better put those wheels or whatever you got up there in gear. The manager of this fire-trap is going to put a business in our keyhole if we don't rustle some rent."

The Doc's big red face is solemn. "I have been some-what disturbed about our ailing finances," he says. "But I have a little operation in mind that I think may result in a quick cure."

I pull off my coat and reach for the bourbon. A couple of minutes later I am feeling better. "What is this caper you have cooked up?" I ask him.

The Doc frowns. "It is not a caper," he says. "I have evolved a scientific method of applying the laws of percentage to your efforts at the racetrack."

"Listen," I tell him. "I am too tired to hear about some system you have dreamed up for beating the races. I hit one winner all afternoon and the chump I hook bets a double sawbuck on him. This nag comes in at eight-to-one and when I move in to collect my commission there is a big Pinkerton standing right beside the chump."

"That is my point exactly," the Doc says. "You are working against the percentage. The Pinkertons are simply an added burden." He taps his fingers against the bottle. "You are trying to pick winners when the percentage is in favor of the losers."

I know the Doc is a good hand with a percentage, but this doesn't make sense. "They don't pay off on losers," I tell him. "Not at this racetrack anyhow."

"We are going to change all that," the Doc says. "If you can pick the losers, I will make them pay off."

"I will pick you losers until the cows come home," I tell him.

"Excellent," he says. He hitches up his chair and lowers his voice. "Listen carefully, pony boy. This is going to be the most delicate operation we have attempted. We can't make any mistakes."

THE FIRST time I catch sight of J. Hamilton Wilkins, he is listening to a party by the name of the Preacher. This

Wilkins' mouth is open and I can see he hardley believes what is going on before his eyes.

Preacher is not connected with any churches so far as I know, but he is called the Preacher because he has a long, sad face and always wears a little black string tie around his neck.

J. Hamilton Wilkins is a short party about fifty years old with a round face and a little feather in his hat. He is paying close attention to what the Preacher is saying so I figure he has not been around very long and probably has a wallet full of crisp banknotes.

Sure enough, after the Preacher talks to him for a while Wilkins takes out his leather and hands the Preacher what looks to me like a crisp banknote. I cannot see just how large this banknote is but I figure it is ten or maybe twenty, because the Preacher takes it over and puts it in at one of the mutuel windows. If it is any larger, say a half-a-yard or better, I know the Preacher will not invest it in whatever nag he has been telling Wilkins about, but will put it in his own pants pocket and run out the gate with it.

After the ponies get away I move over and stand close to Wilkins on the opposite side from where the Preacher is standing. The Preacher gives me a dirty look but I do not pay any attention as I am listening carefully to what Wilkins is saying as the horses come down the stretch. He is yelling: "Come on, nine!"

Well, this number nine horse is not coming on. In fact he seems to be going backward, so I peek at the number of the horse that is laying on top. He is number two, and just before he pushes his nose under the wire I yell, "Come on, two," very loud, right in J. Hamilton Wilkins' ear.

Wilkins is startled when I yell in his ear and he turns and looks at me and then turns around again to say something to the Preacher. The Preacher is not there any more, so I figure he has told Wilkins quite a tale to get him to invest in this number nine.

The number two horse was the favorite and when the prices go up on the board I notice that he only pays off three dollars and a few odd pennies for every two dollars invested in him. This is what I have been hoping for so I snort very loud in Wilkins' ear and say: "How lucky I am that I collect ten-to-one just now on this winner."

Wilkins turns and looks at me again and I can tell he is interested in my remark so I give him a big smile. "This will cost that old smarty, Dr. Pierce, one thousand dollars," I say. "It will be a good lesson to him."

Wilkins makes a noise in his throat as though he is trying to get rid of a fishbone. "Pardon me, sir," he says.

"But did I hear you say that you are collecting ten-to-one on the horse that just won this race?"

"That's right," I tell him. "That silly old Dr. Pierce bet me a thousand against a hundred that this number two would not win."

Wilkins has more trouble with the fishbone. "This Dr. Pierce," he says finally. "Is he a bookmaker?"

"Oh, no," I tell him. "It is against the law to make a book on this track. Dr. Pierce is a retired medical man from Chicago and a very respectable citizen. Although," I say, "he is considered a little eccentric by some people because he will bet you a good fat price that almost any horse will not win a race." I stop and laugh. "A few of us have made a very good thing out of Dr. Pierce during this meeting, but he is a stubborn old gentleman and he has more dollars than Heinz has got pickles so he keeps sending it in."

Wilkins laughs too but I can see he is thinking hard. I figure he is about ready so I ask him if he would like to meet Dr. Pierce. He brightens up and comes along quietly.

THE DOC is bellying up to the bar in the clubhouse and he looks very good, at that. He has a sharp crease in his best striped pants and he has rubbed most of the spots off his sway-back coat. He lifts his wide black skimmer and bows when I introduce him to J. Hamilton Wilkins and then he gives me a poke in the ribs.

"You must buy the juleps, you lucky young rascal," he says. "You have just separated me from more of my hard-earned dollars." He smiles at Wilkins. "Mr. Allan is trying to convince me that my theory is untenable." He shakes his head. "Mr. Allan has separated me from about six thousand dollars in the past ten days, but his success is based on the vagaries of chance and cannot continue."

The juleps arrive and Wilkins picks one up and buries his nose in the foliage while he thinks it over. Finally he comes up for air. "If I understood correctly, Doctor," he says, "you are willing to lay generous odds that a particular horse will not win a particular race, regardless of the handicapper's rating."

"Exactly," the Doc tells him. "My theory is based on the premise that most of the horses in a race do not win. Of course," he adds, "I reserve the right to refuse a bet on a horse that does not fall into my category of horses who cannot win."

Wilkins goes back into the foliage to think this over and I figure it is time to make my play so I give the Doc the office.

The Doc reaches into his clothes and draws out a fat leather. I know it is stuffed with folded newspaper but I can't help being a little impressed, at that. I like to look at a fat wallet. I wait until I am sure Wilkins has had a good gander at the wallet, too, and then I raise my hand.

"No, Doctor," I say. "Do not pay me the cash now. Just hold it and add it to my account as usual. I like those double odds and maybe I will get a red-hot winner and bet it all and put you out of business."

The Doc chuckles and puts the wallet back in his pocket. "I am afraid you will have to build up a larger balance than you have at present if you expect to put me out of business," he says. He smiles at Wilkins. "I have a little arrangement with Mr. Allan. If he leaves his winnings with me I give him double odds on his bets. For example, the winner of this last race was only five-to-one against in my book, but Mr. Allan got ten-to-one."

Wilkins stares at the Doc with his mouth open and some of his julep I just bounce six bits for drools down his chin. I can see he thinks the Doc is a very eccentric old gentlemen indeed.

The Doc smiles when he sees this look on Wilkins and he moves in for the pitch. "Do you ever wager on the ponies, sir?"

Wilkins gets his mouth closed and nods. "Why, yes," he says. "I sometimes take a little flutter just to pass the time away." He stands there for a minute. His brain is working so fast you can almost hear it click. The favorites have been coming in very regular at this meeting and the prices have been very short for that reason. I can see the figures going around in Wilkins' skull and I decide to give him a lead.

"How about this number three horse in the next race?" I ask the Doc. "What does your little book say about him?"

The Doc pulls out a notebook and puts on his cheaters with the black ribbon on them. He hides the notebook under his hand and takes a peak at it. "Number three," he says. "That is a bay gelding called Tick Tack." He turns over a couple of pages. "Yes," he says. "Tick Tack is in the proper column. I will lay six-to-one that he will not win."

"That's fine," I tell him. "I will take five hundred dollars' worth of that. Slim Barkley is training Tick Tack and Slim Barkley is a very smart young man around a racehorse. I figure he is due to win."

The Doc makes a note in his book. "Of course," he says, "I will extend you the usual courtesy of double odds, so I am betting six thousand dollars against your five hundred." He puts the book back in his pocket and takes off his cheaters.

WILKINS' MOUTH is open again and I can see he hardly believes what is going on before his eyes. He glances up at the board on the clubhouse wall and Tick Tack is no better than even money with several minutes to go before post time. He reaches for his wallet.

"Just a moment, Doctor," he says. "If you have no objection I would like to go along with Mr. Allan on this Tick Tack, just to while away the time."

The Doc smiles and shakes his head. "I will be happy to oblige you," he says. "But you look like a man of mature intelligence. Surely you would not invest your money in a proposition so directly opposed to the laws of scientific probability?"

This is quite a mouthful, even for the Doc, and I can see it goes down very well with Wilkins. He gives a little laugh and draws his leather. "I am just a plain businessman on a vacation, Doctor. This is recreation for me." He pulls a couple of yards out of his wallet and holds them out. "Please put my two hundred in with Mr. Allan's five hundred." He hesitates. "Of course I understand that you will only give me six-to-one as I have no balance on your books."

The Doc shakes his head again and glances down the bar. "Perhaps you would prefer to have the bartender hold the stakes? After all, I am a stranger."

I get a little nervous when the Doc makes this play as I know the Doc does not have any twelve hundred in his clothes, or even twelve dollars, but I don't have to worry. Wilkins is only too willing to get on the Doc's balance sheet and dip into this double-odds gravy. He pushes the banknotes at the Doc. "I will be honored if you will hold the stakes," he says.

The Doc's fingers are curling at the ends but he makes a slow reach for the banknotes and shoves them in his pocket nice and easy. He turns back to his mint julep. "I never watch the ponies run," he tells Wilkins, "but I will be here to deaden your agony with another julep after Tick Tack loses."

I watch this Tick Tack on his way to the post and I know we are all set. The jock is a good strong boy and I know that even if the boy's arms drop off Slim Barkley would run out on the track and hit Tick Tack in the head with an axe before he would let him win at even money or less. In fact I figure that if any horse this Slim Barkley trains ever won a race at less than five-to-one, Slim Barkley would shoot the horse and himself in the head with a gun.

I notice Wilkins is looking around at the crowd behind us with a frown on his face. I get ready for a quick duck in case it is a Pinkerton he is looking for but he turns back to me and taps his fingers on the rail. "I cannot understand it," he says. "My daughter promised to meet me here before this race."

This doesn't sound so good. I have been hoping that Wilkins is here alone as I prefer to operate on chumps who do not have dames hanging around them. I asks if his whole family is with him.

"All the family I have is my daughter," he tells me. "My wife passed away about a year ago."

I feel better when I hear this as a young dame is not apt to hang around her old man much. I settle down to enjoy the race.

This Tick Tack breaks about fourth and the jock takes him so wide on the first turn that I think he is going to swing right over the fence and out of sight. By the time they hit the back-stretch the other boys have him shut off so tight he can't get through with a shoe-horn.

When they turn for home the boy takes Tick Tack wide again and then knocks on him a couple of times with his bat. He shoves his nose up in time for fourth money which will take care of his feed bill for that month, but as most of the people in the stands have invested in Tick Tack to win or at least show and they do not care about any feed bills except their own, they are quite upset and groan very loud.

I groan too, right in Wilkins' ear, but he doesn't groan back. Wilkins is being a good loser. He grins and says: "Well, we will collect those juleps from the doctor."

I don't know whether I like this attitude or not. Sometimes when you get a chump that is a good loser he goes home and forgets about it. If they are a little upset they are more apt to stay in and pitch.

WHILE WE are walking toward the bar I notice a black-haired young dame with very bright blue eyes coming our way. She has pink cheeks and is not a bad type so I look her over carefully. She does not give me a tumble but marches up to Wilkins.

"Where have you been, Daddy?" she says. "I have been looking for you." She sniffs a couple of times. "You have been drinking whiskey. You know what the doctor said."

Wilkins grins at her. "I have a new doctor now," he tells her. "He prescribes mint juleps." He turns to me. "This is my daughter, Arabella, Mr. Allan."

Arabella gives me a big smile but I can see she is not much interested, which suits me as I am not interested in dames with male relatives around the premises. She tags along to the bar with us and Wilkins puts her away with the Doc. The Doc is quite a hand for dames when he has the price and he spreads it on Arabella very thick. He buys her one of these pink messes that dames like to drink and raises his glass to Wilkins.

"Now that you have had your little lesson," he says, "I hope you are convinced of the folly of opposing the principles of science."

Wilkins glances at me, then he turns back to the Doc and shakes his head. "I must admit that Tick Tack has backed up your theory," he says. "But I still think it is more fun to pick them and watch them win."

The Doc smiles. "I cannot say that you have spoken like a scholar," he says, "but at least you are a gentleman and a sportsman." He turns to me. "What do you like in the next race, Mr. Allan?"

I nearly break my wrist getting my program out. "Number eight," I tell him. "In my opinion he can't lose." I look at the Doc. "Will you give me an argument on this number eight?"

The Doc takes a peek into his little book and nods. "Four-to-one," he says, very snappy.

Wilkins draws his leather. "I will take another two hundred of that," he says.

The Doc smiles at him and shakes his head. He glances at the dame. "Can't you persuade your father to stop wasting his money on these horses that cannot win?"

Arabella looks at Wilkins and says: "Did you bet on Tick Tack in that last race?"

Wilkins nods.

"Well," she says, "I could have told you that Tick Tack was not going to win. Egbert told me so."

Wilkins' round face gets very stern. "I have told you that I do not care to hear anything that Egbert has to say. In fact I do not care to hear anything about Egbert." He turns to the Doc. "I must apologize for intruding my domestic problems."

Arabella puts her nose up into the air and moves off into the crowd. Her lips are shaking a little and she is stepping like a hackney, so I figure she's upset.

The Doc takes the two bills Wilkins holds out to him and shoves them in his pocket. He is looking at Wilkins very hard and I can see he smells an angle. He shakes his head and sighs.

"I must confess the young people puzzle me nowadays," he says. "They have no respect for the judgment of their elders."

Wilkins nods. "This Egbert is a sore subject with me," he says. "I have never met him and I do not intend to meet him. I do not approve of his method of making a living. He is no better than a parasite."

The Doc slips one hand in his pocket in case the banknotes try to crawl out into the air again. "I suppose this Egbert has designs on your bank account?"

"Yes," Wilkins tells him. "And he is very brazen about it. Arabella has been pestering me for a week to let her have some of the money her mother left in trust for her. Arabella will not receive this money until she is twenty-five, two years from now." He shakes his head. "I think I would be very foolish to give her ten thousand dollars so this Egbert can set up in business for himself."

NUMBER EIGHT loses, right on schedule, and so does every other nag that Wilkins takes on. By the time we get back to the hotel the Doc has taken the newspaper out of his wallet and thrown it away. I am very sassy to the manager when he speaks about the back rent.

Well, I have been here and there and I have seen some high-rollers in my time but I never run into anyone who sends it along like this J. Hamilton Wilkins. We go into the last week of the meeting with about seven thousand of Wilkins' dollars tucked away in the Doc's wallet.

Arabella shows up for a drink once in a while and although she knows that her old man is taking this beating it does not seem to bother her. She does not stay around the clubhouse much and I figure she is snuggling up in a corner somewhere with this Egbert. Later on it turns out I am right.

One evening the Doc has a big smile on his face when I meet him outside the gate and while we are putting on the steaks he tells me that Arabella has asked him if he will accommodate her with a small bet on a horse the next day. He says she made him promise not to tell her old man she was playing the ponies.

"Well," I tell him, "any horse Arabella picks is not likely to do much damage. If she wishes to donate a few dimes I think we should accommodate her."

I am not so sure about this the next day. The nag Arabella plays bobs down in front and while he is even money on the board the Doc has given Arabella five-to-one. She bet two yards so she is into us for a grand. She draws down the two hundred and tells the Doc to hold the thousand as she may wish to bet again and she would like double odds.

I tell the Doc he had better pay her off and let her go but he laughs at me. "We are not out anything to date," he says, "and as tomorrow is the last day of the meeting Arabella will have to step fast to collect that thousand."

I get out to the track early next morning. Wilkins has a very determined look on his face when he meets us in the clubhouse before the first race. The Doc has told me he figured Wilkins would try very hard to come out even on this last round and sure enough he bangs in five hundred on the first heat. The nag runs out and Wilkins belts in another five yards on the second race.

Just before the third race I catch sight of Arabella going into the bar and I take Wilkins by the arm and steer him over to the saddling-paddock to look at a nag I have heard some nice things about. Although they are not the same things I tell Wilkins about.

The swipe that rubs this nag is an old pal of mine and he tells me that morning that there is a boat-race on and this nag is to run in bandages. Of course it is perfectly proper to run a horse in bandages but when they put the bandages on this particular nag they intend to draw the strings up very tight around his leg, and along about the quarter pole the nag is going to find out that he is not getting the circulation he is accustomed to. It is amazing how a racehorse will slow down when he finds out he is not getting circulation.

In a little while I see Arabella coming back out of the bar so I take Wilkins in to make his donation. He sends another five bills along on this bargain in the bandages.

When Wilkins heads for the rail I stay behind for a few seconds and ask the Doc how he makes out with Arabella.

"Very fine," he tells me. "Arabella has directed me to invest the entire thousand dollars in the very horse-that initiated our pleasant association with her father, this Tick Tack."

I look up at the board. "Well," I tell him, "the investors and the handicappers still have faith in Tick Tack. I see he is even money and dropping fast. Slim Barkley will not send him in to win at such a ridiculous price."

"That is exactly why I gave Arabella the special rate of ten-to-one," the Doc says.

I HAVE to hang on to the fence for a minute as the nags come under the wire in that third race but I soon recover and head for the clubhouse at a dead run.

There is only one way in and out of the bar and just as I gallop up I see Arabella scuttle through the door. By the time I arrive she is inside and has the Doc cornered. I move up behind Arabella and am considering the chances of putting the slug on her and ducking out fast when I notice Cap Donovan, the boss Pinkerton around the track, standing near the door. I also notice this trainer, Slim Barkley, standing down the bar and looking at Arabella with a great deal of interest. I am pretty excited but I find time to wonder what he is doing in the clubhouse when his horse Tick Tack has just won a race down on the track.

The Doc is a little pale around the gills but he gives Arabella a big smile. "You are a very fortunate young lady," he says. He wiggles his fingers at me to close in on the other side of the dame. "I believe you should buy Mr. Allan and myself a julep."

I can't figure whether the Doc is just stalling or if he has something in mind. Whatever it is, he forgets it right away when I give him the office that there is a policeman present. He gets a little paler but he hangs onto his smile. "Your father is coming in the door," he tells Arabella.

She squeals and hops up and down. "Look, Daddy," she yells at Wilkins. "I have just won ten thousand dollars from Dr. Pierce."

Wilkins bugs out his eyes until I am afraid they are going to roll down his cheeks. "Ten thousand!" he says. "How did it happen?"

Arabella's cheeks are pinker than ever. "Egbert planned it all," she says. "I have been trying to tell you how clever he is but you wouldn't listen. When I told him about Dr.

Pierce giving such marvelous odds on favorites Egbert told me just what to do. He gave me two hundred to bet on a horse yesterday that he knew was going to win and then he told me to leave the thousand I won with the doctor and bet it all on Tick Tack today."

Wilkins gets his breath back. He looks a little sad. "I suppose I had better meet this Egbert," he says.

Arabella puts her arms around Wilkins and says: "You will like Egbert, Daddy. I know you will." She holds out her pink palm to the Doc and I have to turn my head away. I can't stand it to watch all that lettuce floating out of the Doc's wallet. I do some quick figuring. The Doc has just about enough to cover the eleven grand he has to hand Arabella. We will not have enough left to even spring us out of the hotel. I am very sorry I was so sassy with the manager.

Arabella crams the wad into her handbag and tells the barkeep to set up the juleps. I almost ask him to put arsenic in mine.

I'll hand it to the Doc, he has plenty of moxie. His color is coming back already and he lifts his glass and says that he hopes Arabella and her Egbert will be very happy.

"I am going to bring Egbert over right away to meet all you nice people," she says, "I know you will be glad to meet Egbert, Mr. Allan. He tells me he has known you for many years."

Well, when I think it over afterward I realize I should not have been surprised when Arabella comes back hanging onto Slim Barkley's arm. Nobody but Slim Barkley could be responsible for Tick Tack's win. And I have been around for some time, but even the Doc does not know that my first name is Marmaduke.

THE DOCTOR'S DITCH

IT LOOKS LIKE A VERY FANCY
PITCH INDEED WHEN DOC PIERCE
GETS HIMSELF APPOINTED
PRESIDENT OF THE SPUYTENHAM
BOARD OF HEALTH... JUST
THE JOB FOR A MEDICO WITH
THE DOC'S VAST EXPERIENCE
PEDDLING RATTLESNAKE OIL
AROUND THE CARNIVAL CIRCUIT.

THESE NIGHT-CLUB mice along Broadway have been taking big nibbles at my wallet but I am still holding plenty when the doc's wire arrives.

I can't make any sense out of this message but I know it is from the Doc as it comes from this town of Spuytenham where he holes up after we make the big score at Belmont Park.

The wire says: NEED HELP ON WELFARE PROJECT SEWERS HERE RUNNING PURE GOLD, and it is signed HIGHBALL so I know he wishes me to join him immediately.

I grab the first train out of Grand Central and on the way I try to figure what kind of action the Doc has stirred up in this Spuytenham. I spend a couple of days with him when he first backs into the place and in my book it is strictly no dice. The town is inhabited by a bunch of old guys and dames that wobble around like spavined selling-platers and if you see a couple of people together on the street the chances are one of them is holding the other one up.

The Doc is quite taken with the place, however, and he tells me he has his eye on it for some time. He claims there is more dollars per citizen in Spuytenham than any other town in the country and I am willing to believe this, as all

these old guys and dames live in houses the size of tobac-
co-barns with gardens and flunkies all over the premises.

I also know the Doc can run up a score in any kind of
going where people with dollars are around. But before you
can score you got to have action. And the time I spend in
Spuytenham I don't see enough action to stir up a sweat
in a nervous two-year-old.

THE DOC meets me at the station with a grin on his
big red face. He is sharpened up in a new sway-back coat
and he has a press in his striped pants that will cut washers
off the rear end of an alligator.

"I was certain that wire would bring you at the gallop,"
he says. "I purposely couched it in ambiguous terms to
arouse your curiosity."

I'm glad to see the Doc, at that. "Well, I'm here," I tell
him. "What's the caper?"

The Doc frowns. "I have a little plan in mind that will
be of great benefit to this community and at the same time
make us wealthy beyond the dreams of avarice," he says. "It
pains me to hear you refer to this benevolent undertaking
in such uncouth terms."

"O.K.," I tell him. "Call it anything you like, but hurry
up and tell me the part about where we get rich. I am still
carrying five grand in my pants pocket and I need another
five to keep me from tipping over sideways."

The Doc grins. "I am pleased to hear you are holding
that heavy," he says. "The initial expenses on this pitch
have been greater than I anticipated." He jerks his thumb
at a long black heap in the street outside. "That glittering
mechanism rents for five bills per month, cash in advance,
and that repulsive object in the front seat is Higgins, my

"Good-morning, Millicent,"
says the Doc. "We are just taking
a few things to the cleaner's."

chauffeur. Higgins and this character he is married to set
me back another two hundred."

I don't get it. "If this Higgins is a wrong gee, why slip
him two yards a month?" I ask him. "Why don't you give
him the heave?"

The Doc shakes his head. "I had difficulty renting an
establishment in keeping with my position in this community," he says. "Higgins and his mate were included in the
deal I made with Miss Millicent Baxter, the owner of my
current residence." He gets a look on his face I have seen
before. "Millicent is a fine woman," he says. "Her grandfather put the arm on many a dollar in his day and she owns
plenty of property and is highly regarded."

I don't like it. "I suppose you have been putting in plenty
of work on this Baxter," I tell him.

The Doc cackles. "I will admit that I made several attempts to establish a warmer relationship," he says. "But Millicent's heart belongs to a retired pedagogue named Professor Starbuck."

"Well," I tell him, "I hope this professor keeps a tight curb on her. Every time you start tampering with some old bag of rags you get your feet crossed on the turns and we lose money." I take a good look at the automobile. "You are certainly throwing a front in this burg," I tell him. "I hope you can cash out."

The Doc glances around and lowers his voice. "I will tell you this much right now, pony boy," he says. "This is no paltry five grand touch. We will walk out of Spuytenham with a hundred thousand in our pants pockets."

I have been in some fast company in my time and I know the Doc can stay on the pace with any of them but I have to admit this sets me back on my hocks. I don't ask any more questions, though, as I know the Doc will not open up until he is ready.

Higgins hauls it out of the seat as we come up and opens the door for us. Up close Higgins is a chunky party with about as much expression on his face as a feedbucket and I can see why the Doc is annoyed at having him around. The Doc likes a laugh once in a while. Especially when he is paying out his own money.

ON THE way to this trap the Doc has rented we pass a gang of dagos pulling hunks out of the street with a steamshovel. The Doc tells Higgins to stop the car and a husky dago who is hollering at the other dagos comes over and shakes hands with us. It turns out his name is Luigi Concato and the Doc claims out loud that Luigi is a smart operator and has the best equipment in the country for tearing up streets and slapping down sewers.

Well, I know there is an angle here or the Doc will not be greasing up this dago. Especially as Luigi is plenty greasy already from what I can see. I also remember what the Doc says in his telegram about the sewers running with gold but the only way I figure you can get gold in a sewer is to poke it into a bank vault. This is back in the days when they still have gold in bank vaults but I know the Doc never touches that kind of a caper.

The Doc sees I am puzzled but he just grins. "Mr. Allen is going to assist us in our little enterprise," he tells Luigi.

Luigi pokes his head and a blast of garlic into the car and cackles in my ear. "We catch plenty good business, me and Doc Pierce," he says.

I don't care much for this. Aside from the way he smells, this Luigi is a big strong dago. I have seen dagos only half his size that made plenty of noise when people took money away from them and I figure if the Doc has designs on Luigi's bankroll we better have the door open for a quick duck.

This trap the Doc has rented has a lot of class, with thick carpets on the floor and a bunch of furniture it would take a crowbar to move. Mrs. Higgins meets us at the door and the Doc puts me away with her as an old business associate. Mrs. Higgins is a nosy dame with big ears and her hair pulled into a tight wad at the back of her collar. She acts like it will cost her four bits if she cracks a smile and from the way she looks at me I figure she will just as soon dust a little arsenic on my pork chops as not.

After we put on the feed-bag the Doc breaks out a bottle of bourbon and we sit in front of the fire and push it back and forth. The Doc waits until he hears the back door close and then he lets out his breath.

"I always feel better after those two zombies have crawled into their lair above the garage," he says.

"Well," I tell him, "Mrs. Higgins is no green hand with a skillet. That was an excellent dinner."

"Yes," he says, "they are an efficient couple although from the looks of the bills I suspect they are playing very close ball with the local merchants. I shall have to work out a little plan for the Higgins family before we leave. I do not approve of people who clip me for a percentage."

I don't care much for this Higgins setup but I feel sorry for them, at that. I would not care to be on the other end of one of the Doc's little plans. "I suppose you have a little plan for this dago gardenia we met on the way over here?"

The Doc nods. "Yes," he says. "Luigi is a vital factor in our immediate future." He pushes the bourbon over to me. "Take a stiff dose, pony boy. I have a surprise for you." He reaches in his clothes and tosses this badge in my lap. It is the prettiest buzzer I ever look at, all gold with *Health Officer* printed across it.

The Doc looks serious. "As President of the Board of Health of Spuytenham," he says, "I hereby appoint you Deputy Health Officer. I am certain you will be an adornment to the office."

I JUST goggle at him and he has to grin. "While you were wallowing in the gilded gutters of the Big Town," he tells me, "I have put myself away with the right people. My landlady, Miss Millicent Baxter, is an influential member of the Town Council. When the retired medical man who headed the Board passed away a few weeks ago, Millicent persuaded me to accept the office."

I have to snicker. "I suppose you told her about the years you peddled rattlesnake oil around the carnivals."

The Doc shakes his head. "Fortunately the matter of my medical background and credentials did not come up," he says. "The office pays no salary but there is a splendid opportunity for the advancement of our bankroll."

I take another look at the badge. "Can I put the arm on somebody with this?" I ask him. "I know a few parties around the racetracks I would enjoy heaving in the cooler."

The Doc shakes his head. "You will function within the legal limits of your office," he says. "Your principal task will be to assure the property-owners of Spuytenham that Luigi is doing an excellent job on the new sewers."

I begin to catch on. "We tell the citizens Luigi is O.K. and Luigi shakes down for a percentage, is that it?"

The Doc nods. "That is a rough outline. As head of the Board of Health I can make it very uncomfortable for Luigi. He has a good contract with the Township and he stands to make a tidy profit if everything goes smoothly."

"But suppose Luigi collects and then refuses to hold still for this payoff?" I ask him.

The Doc grins. "Luigi had to shave his figures very thin to get the contract for laying the mains. He will make his real dough putting in the connections to the houses. Every citizen has to pay for his own connection and each connection is a private contract between Luigi and the property-owner. Luigi figures the connections will gross around two million as all the houses in town are set way back from the street. He has agreed to tack on a modest five per cent for our benefit and he will pay off as each connection is laid in." He pours a big dose of the bourbon and puts it down. "Luigi knows very well that they put people in jail for bribing a public official."

It looks airtight to me. I am a public official. I pin the buzzer on my chest. "Do I look like a G-man?" I ask him.

The Doc shakes his head and laughs. "You look like a fifty-G-man to me, pony boy."

I laugh, too. The Doc is a card.

I SPEND the next couple of days hanging around Luigi and his gang. I am careful to stay on the upwind side and it doesn't take me long to find out what goes. When I'm sure I have the idea I start calling on property-owners and breaking the news about the modern plumbing.

At first I am a little nervous as I figure somebody will want to know how come I am hustling this badge around but it finally dawns on me that I am just like the mailman and the butcher-boy. I am just there.

Every evening I pick up the fresh estimates from Luigi and take them home so the Doc can work them over and tack on our five per cent. We get many a laugh when I tell him how these property-owners scream and carry on when they realize what this program is going to cost them. I can see how this Health Officer dodge is very handy as nobody figures a Health Officer will be up to any larceny and I don't hear any of the taxpayers say they intend to call in another opinion. When I tell them Luigi is their best bet they swallow it right down.

One morning I mope in on this boy friend of the Doc's landlady, Professor Starbuck. The professor is a quiet little guy with sad brown eyes and a mop of white hair. He takes me into a big room with books piled all over the floor and we bat the weather around and have a pleasant little chat for a while.

Finally I pull out the Doc's edition of Luigi's estimate on the plumbing connections and hand it over. The professor's house is set up on a little hill about half a furlong from the street and Luigi claims it will be quite a chore to poke a sewer into it.

The bill comes to about two grand and the professor indignantly mentions the sum right away.

"This is an outrage," he hollers. "Two thousand dollars for a ditch and a few lengths of pipe!" He starts prancing up and down the floor and I have never heard such a big beef from a little guy.

I manage to keep a straight face and after a while he cools out. I give him the quick once-over on how Luigi is on the ground and has the big equipment so he can do the job cheaper than anybody and before I leave I also inform him that the law says he must connect with the main within ninety days.

He opens his mouth to let out another scream when I tell him this but it turns out he is short of breath. I look back while I am easing out the door and he is staring at this paper like he expects it to stab him with a knife.

The Doc shakes his head when I tell him about the professor that evening. "My sympathies are with Professor Starbuck," he says. "I understand all the professor has in the world is his little home and a modest pension from the University. He would be wise to let Miss Millicent Baxter put the clamp on him. Everybody in town knows that Millicent would like to be Mrs. Starbuck."

We are parked in the Doc's bedroom and he has a stack of Luigi's estimates on the desk in front of him. He frowns and looks at me. "Have you been meddling with these papers?"

Of course I tell him I have no head for figures except on a form-sheet or the kind you put in mink coats so why would I be fooling with these estimates.

The Doc looks a little worried. "Someone has disarranged these estimates," he says. "I don't like the idea."

"That Higgins and his wife are always gum-shoeing around on these carpets," I tell him. "Maybe they take a peek into your desk once in a while."

"That is probably it," he says. "I shall certainly have to pay a little attention to that pair before we leave." He picks up a thick bundle. "Speaking of Millicent," he says, "here are the figures on her various properties. She is the largest property-owner in town so naturally I have given her special service. I have upped her figures just a trifle over the usual five per cent as I consider the rental I am paying on this dump is exorbitant."

I take a look at the estimates. Luigi tells me that some parts of Spuytenham are solid rock and from the looks of these figures Baxter's houses are sitting on granite. The bill runs nearly nineteen grand before the Doc adds a flat two thousand to it. "Well," I tell him, "I will hand it to you. You are really putting the clip on this bag of rags."

The Doc grins. "I understand this old grandfather who gathered up her dollars was an unscrupulous rogue. It will be an act of common justice to air off some of those moldy old bills."

I MOVE in on this Baxter bag the next morning. She turns out to be a rangy old dame with plenty of daylight under her and a sunburned face. I flash the buzzer and she gives me a big smile.

"You must be the young man Doctor Pierce spoke about," she says. "Doctor Pierce said he thought we were fortunate to secure your services."

Before I can come up with a kickback on this she starts flapping her hand at somebody out in the street. I turn around and at first all I see is Luigi and a bunch of his dagos who are marking out the next place he intends to yank up. Then I notice Professor Starbuck standing on the upwind side of Luigi and speaking to him with a very serious look on his face. I figure the professor is telling Luigi how unhappy he is about the cost of the new plumbing and I have a hard time to keep from snickering.

The professor smiles and waves back at Baxter and I notice her brown cheeks get very pink. When we get in the house I put in a couple of quick boosts for the professor and then I draw the estimates on her. I figure I better get into the pitch right away before she cools out.

"Doctor Pierce is greatly concerned about the cost of these new sanitary facilities to the property-owners," I tell her. "He has directed me to check up on the contractor's work and also to make certain that his charges are held to a minimum."

Baxter nods and glances at the papers. I notice her eyes open very wide and I get set for the screeching and bellowing but she takes it quietly.

"This is a large sum of money," she says. "I had no idea when this program was instituted that it would prove so expensive."

I slip her another helping. "Of course," I tell her, "the increase in property values will more than offset the cost of the program, not to mention the value from a standpoint of public health." I know this is a good spiel as the Doc has taught it to me very, carefully.

Baxter nods again and stuffs the estimates into a drawer. She gives me a smile and says: "How long have you been engaged in health work, Mr. Allen?"

I am all set for this one, too.

"My dear old mother slaved and sacrificed to put me through medical school," I tell her. "During my second year she became very ill and I had to return home. Since she passed on Doctor Pierce has been very kind to me and has promised to assist me in finishing my medical education."

"I imagine Doctor Pierce is well equipped to help you with your education," Baxter says. She leans forward and looks at me very serious. "Tell me, Mr. Allen," she says, "how long is the period of isolation for a case of clavicle?"

I can't afford to hesitate. "That depends on the case," I tell her. "Sometimes it takes a couple of months."

Baxter nods and picks up the telephone. "Get me Doctor Pierce's residence," she tells the operator. When the Doc answers she says: "I think you had better come over immediately, Doctor. Mr. Allen is having a little trouble explaining certain things to me."

Well, I know I am out of line somewhere but I figure my play is to dummy up until the Doc gets there. Baxter does not push me around but starts telling me about the trouble her gardener is having with a new lawn he just puts in. It is quite a relief to me when the Doc arrives.

He has a big smile on his face but he shoots a quick look at me before he grabs Baxter by both mitts and I know he is worried. I rub my chin with my left hand to show him I have not spilled anything and I can almost feel him relax.

"Well, my dear," he says to Baxter, "what are you bothering your pretty head about this morning?"

If Baxter ever looks in a mirror she knows her head is not pretty at all, unless maybe it is on a mule, but she gives a little giggle and her cheeks get pink so the Doc serves her another portion quick. "I do not like to see a charming woman concern herself with dull matters of finance," he says. "I hope you are not distressed over the expense of our new program?"

Baxter giggles again and gets her hands loose. "My attorneys handle my business affairs," she says. "But I am a little curious about your friend Mr. Allen. Mr. Allen told me a tall story about being an ex-medical student but he could not answer a question I asked him."

WELL, I am not too pleased with all this "Mr. Allen" business and I start to say something about it but the Doc gives me the office to stay dummied up.

"I owe you an apology, Millicent," he says. "I am afraid I have been guilty of a slight deception." He moves across the room and sits down as close to Baxter as he can get without crawling into her lap. "Mr. Allen is the only son of a dear old friend," he tells her. "I take a fatherly interest in the boy and I have tried to help him over the thornier portions of life's pathway." He shakes his head and looks at me as though I had just broke a leg and he is figuring on shooting me. "Mr. Allen is like his late parent," he says. "He is too proud to accept charity but he seems to lack the aptitude for acquiring this world's goods. I thought the opportunity of serving this community under my supervision and of earning a modest wage at the same time would develop his confidence and perhaps equip him to face the world with greater success."

Of course the Doc knows very well that my old man is still driving a truck in Brooklyn but he is mopping his eyes with his handkerchief before he is halfway through this spiel. I am about ready to slip myself a dime and Baxter looks as though she is going to park me on her knee any minute.

The Doc puts his handkerchief away and smiles at Baxter. "I must take the responsibility for the harmless fiction Mr. Allen related to you," he says. He shakes his head. "Feminine intuition is a marvelous thing," he says. "Especially when it is coupled with unusual intelligence."

From there in it is a breeze. When we leave, Baxter pats me on the head and tells me not to worry. She will not divulge my little secret.

We get back to the Doc's house and I tell him about the question Baxter asked me. He laughs until I think he is going to split his white waistcoat. "Clavicle," he says. "Clavicle is the medical term for your collarbone. Millicent is a pretty smart old pelter at that." He laughs again. "Anyhow I steered her off the sewer connections. Those attorneys of hers will have to find a steam-shovel in their briefcase if they expect to check on Luigi's prices. I think Millcent is put away in good shape." He shakes his head at me. "She will probably be over with a plate of cookies for you in the morning."

"Well," I tell him, "I will eat the cookies and come back for more. Maybe Millicent will adopt me or something and then I will not have to sit around and hear you knock my old man."

That night when Luigi comes by with the day's batch of estimates he looks worried. "This Professor Starbuck," he tells us. "He raises plenty hell today. He thinks we charge him too much for the hookup."

The Doc laughs and pours Luigi a dose of bourbon. "The professor and I see alike," he says. "I agree that we are charging him too much," He pokes Luigi in the ribs. "Can you think of anything the professor can do about it?"

Luigi laughs too, but he still looks worried. "Old lady Baxter," he says. "She ask me plenty questions, too."

The Doc grins at me. "Did she ask you about clavicles?" Luigi shakes his head. "Just about the sewer," he says.

The Doc starts Luigi out the door as the bourbon is still running second to the garlic and the room is getting thick. "Don't worry, partner," he says. "You keep poking that pipe down the street. The Board of Health will take care of everything."

"Sure," Luigi says. "Sure. You take care of me, I take care of you."

A COUPLE of days later I am up early. It is a habit I form around the tracks where you have to clock those beetles yourself if you want to believe anything. I mope down to the kitchen and there is no ham frying on the stove.

There is no Mrs. Higgins either. In fact there is not even Mr. Higgins and the car is gone from the garage. I gallop up to the Doc's room as I figure there is something wrong. The Doc takes one look at his desk and starts getting into his pants.

"Pack up quick, pony boy," he says. "We are lamming out of here."

"What's the panic?" I ask him.

"The desk," he tells me. "The estimates are gone. That blackguard Higgins has sold us out."

We are on our way down the stairs with our suitcases when Baxter walks in the front door. Higgins and three other husky flunkies are standing behind her. They don't look friendly.

The Doc sets down his suitcase. "Good-morning, Millicent," he says smoothly. "We are just taking a few things to the cleaner's."

Baxter looks at him. Her eyes are very bright. "But you are not taking the people of this town to the cleaner's," she says grimly.

She turns to the flunkies. "Wait outside," she tells them. "I won't need you after all." Her lip curls in a nasty way. "Step into the living-room, Doctor Pierce, or whatever your name is."

The Doc bows. "After you, my dear," he says.

He places Baxter in a chair and stands looking down at her. "I underestimated you, Millicent," he says. He smiles at her. "What are your plans? Do you intend to call in the police?" He shakes his head. "After all, Millicent, we have done nothing illegal."

Baxter tries to scowl at him but she has to smile. "You are an unprincipled rascal," she says, "but you are an amusing rascal."

She leans forward and looks the Doc right in the eyes. "I could make it very unpleasant for you, but I will let you leave town unmolested on one condition."

The Doc's voice is soft. "And the condition?"

Baxter's face gets pink but she speaks firmly. "You two thieves are going to pay Professor Starbuck ten thousand dollars cash."

The Doc grins. "I see. If Professor Starbuck has a bankroll of his own he will not be so frightened of your bankroll. Is that it?"

Baxter nods. "That's it exactly." She hesitates for a minute. "You are a very understanding person, Doctor Pierce," she says. "It is a shame you have chosen the path you follow."

The Doc turns to me.

"I can produce half of the ten grand," he says. "Will you put in the other five, pony boy?"

This doesn't make sense to me. I get up. "Listen, Doc," I tell him. "Let us put the slug on this old bag and lam out of here. I will take my chances with those clowns she has parked outside."

The Doc shakes his head and he has a funny look on his face. "I'll scrape up another five thousand for you, pony boy," he says. "Do this for the old man. Shake it down."

Well, the Doc and I have been around together a long time. "O.K.," I tell him. "It is in the bottom of my keester. You dig it out. The operation is too painful for me."

PROFESSOR STARBUCK is a little puzzled but he doesn't hold back when the Doc hands him the ten grand. I have been thinking it over and I remember what a tough dago Luigi is. I am pleased to be getting out of town without a bunch of shiv slashes in my hide. Luigi is going to be very upset when he finds out we have departed.

The Doc is smooth. "The Town Council has instructed me to hand you this retainer for your services as a consultant during the coming fiscal year," he says graciously.

Professor Starbuck puts the arm on the dough. "I will endeavor to furnish counsel that will justify this handsome fee," he says.

The Doc bows back at him and we edge out the door. Before the professor closes it the Doc asks him a question. "What subject did you teach at the University, Professor?"

Professor Starbuck looks somewhat surprised.

"Why," he says, "I thought everybody knew I headed the Department of Engineering."

THE DOCTOR'S FEE

"I WILL BE PROUD TO SHELTER YOU UNDER MY ANCESTRAL ROOF TREE, YOUR EXCELLENCY," SAID "OPERATIVE" SPROCKLE TO THE DOC. SURE, THE LITTLE GUY WAS AS NUTTY AS A FRUITCAKE, BUT HE CAME FROM THE "WOOLEN MILL" SPROCKLES, OWNED A HOUSE AND GROUNDS LIKE THE INFIELD AT HIALEAH AND HAD A FIFTY-GRAND LETTUCE BED SPROUTING IN HIS SAFE DEPOSIT BOX....

T IS a bright moonlight night and I set the Doc's suitcase down while I read this signboard. The Doc is laying about four lengths back and I can hear him wheezing.

"It is only two miles to Sprockleburg," I tell him.

The Doc parts the tails of his swayback coat, sits on a big rock and fans himself with his black skimmer. "And when we arrive in Sprockleburg," he says, very sour, "where will we be then?"

I am not feeling too chipper myself. We do not have a thin dime in our pants pockets and all the clothes I have are on my back. I have to drop my suitcase when this house detective gains on us while we are leaving the last hotel.

"Well," I tell him, "maybe we can find a hockshop in Sprockleburg and soak your keester for the price of a plate of ham and eggs."

The Doc shakes his head. "All of our worldly assets are in that suitcase," he says. "We must retain possession of it at any cost."

"O.K.," I tell him. "Maybe a couple of days on short rations will trim down that haybelly you are packing around." I reach down for the suitcase when I catch this movement in the bushes.

The bushes rustle and a guy slides
out into the road behind the Doc.

"Don't look now," I tell him, "but there is some kind of wild life right behind you, ready to pounce."

The Doc jumps to his feet and even in the moonlight I can see his face is whiter than his vest, which hasn't got so much dust on it, at that.

"What!" he hollers. "Where?"

I have to laugh. The Doc has as much moxie as the next guy, but he is no Daniel Boone and it is dark there in the bushes.

The next second I let out a yelp myself. The bushes rustle again and a guy slides out into the road about a yard from the Doc. The Doc is packing plenty of weight for his age but he makes it across the road in one jump. I am right with him.

THIS PARTY that comes out of the bushes is a slim young guy with his hat turned up all the way around. We stand there looking at each other for a minute and I begin to feel foolish.

The Doc puts his skimmer on his head. "Good-evening, sir," he says. He moves across the road toward this young guy and I move with him in case he has an idea of searching this party.

The young guy is looking at the Doc with his eyes bugged out so you could knock them off with a baseball bat. He takes off his hat and makes a low bow.

"This is a great surprise, Your Excellency," he says. He peeks around at the bushes and steps close to the Doc. "Have no fear," he says. "I will not betray your identity." He takes another look around. "The enemy agents are asleep, but I never sleep."

"That is splendid," the Doc says. "And whom have I the honor of addressing?"

The young guy stands up very straight and salutes. "Operative Sprockle reporting for duty, sir," he says very snappy.

The Doc glances up at the sign beside the road. "Sprockle?" he says.

The young guy nods. "Bedford Sprockle." He puts his finger on his lips. "Sprockleburg is swarming with enemy agents," he says. "But now that you are here our little group will function efficiently."

Of course by this time I realize that Bedford does not have all his buttons. I pick up the suitcase. "O.K., Your Excellency," I tell the Doc. "You stay here and play G-man with this Operative. I will be getting down the road toward the bright lights of Sprockleburg."

The Doc pays no attention to me. He takes Bedford's mitt and pumps it up and down. "This is a fortunate encounter," he says. He points at me. "This is Colonel Allan, my Chief of Staff. We were set upon by enemy agents and robbed of all our funds." He points at the suitcase. "Only Colonel Allan's heroism saved the despatch case with the important documents in it." He shakes his head. "Poor Colonel Allan lost all his uniforms," he says.

I get a snicker out of this as the only uniform I ever owned is when I am a bellhop back in Brooklyn but I begin to see the Doc has something in mind. "Yes," I tell Bedford. "And furthermore we are tired and hungry."

Bedford makes me a bow. "I will be proud to shelter you under my ancestral rooftree," he says. "I live alone except for a trusted manservant. No one will know you are my guests."

It is only about a mile to Bedford's house but it takes us an hour to get there as Bedford insists we go cross-country and hide behind every bush we come to. The country is pretty well bushed over and I am all tuckered out when we make the front door.

BEDFORD'S HOUSE is a classy trap and the grounds around it are dolled up like the infield at Hialeah. I begin to think we have landed on our feet, unless somebody comes along and drops a net over Bedford.

He makes us turn our coat collars up and pull our hats down over our eyes before he rings the bell. After a while a tall party in a monkey suit with a deadpan puss that will fit any poker game in the country opens the door. Bedford pushes us in quick and slaps the door shut like there is a sheriff on the threshold. He reaches out and pulls the Doc's hat up off his eyes.

"The hour has struck," he says. "This is His Excellency in person."

The tall guy bows. "My name is Wigginton, Your Excellency," he says. "I am Mr. Bedford's butler." He slips the Doc a big wink. "Mr. Bedford has been anxiously anticipating your arrival."

Well, I can't make any sense out of this set-up, but the inside of this trap is even more tasty than the outside. Somebody has spent a lot of dough on the premises and I know the Doc will insist on sticking around to find out if there is any left. Anyhow, I figure we can't lose.

Bedford puts me away with the butler as Colonel Allan, the Chief of Staff, and then he bustles around putting our hats away and bowing us upstairs to the bedrooms. These rooms have thick carpets on the floor and bunks about the size of haystacks, only softer.

When I come out of the shower I find Wigginton in the room. He has my suit over his arm and is placing another suit on the bed.

"I took the liberty of laying out one of Mr. Bedford's lounge tweeds and some fresh linen for you, sir," he says. "I will press your clothes and return them in the morning." He lowers his voice. "Mr. Bedford is suffering from a slight mental aberration," he says. "I appreciate your gentlemen's kindness in humoring his fancies." His dead-pan parts in a smile and he goes out the door.

I get dressed and go into the Doc's room. He has broken out his extra striped pants and his spare white vest and he looks O.K. Bedford is about my size and the lounge tweed is a pretty good fit. The Doc takes a look at it and whistles.

"That suit cost somebody about a hundred and fifty checkers," he says. "I think we are very fortunate." He tiptoes to the door and looks up and down the hall. When he comes back he speaks in my ear, very low: "I have not yet figured out a play for Bedford," he tells me, "but I have a feeling there is a chance to score here. This place smells of money."

"Well," I tell him, "when you see this chance, give me the office and I will go along."

We put on the feed bag with Bedford and it turns out that Wigginton is better than a raw hand with a skillet. The Doc stows away enough provisions for a dozen guys and I catch up on these meals I have been postponing.

Between bites Bedford tells us that his family has owned woolen mills in Sprockleburg for many years, although he has no truck with the business personally. He is a nice kid and so far as I can figure out he is O.K. in the head except for this Operative business.

After we have taken on all the groceries we can hold we go into the library and Bedford breaks out a jug of bourbon. The Doc splashes a liberal dose for himself and I take a fair-sized snort but I notice Bedford just touches the bottom of the glass with the whiskey and fills it up with water so I figure he is no lush.

The Doc talks to him about this and that and I know he is fishing for an opening, but he is not getting very far. I begin to nod and am just thinking about this soft bunk upstairs when there is a loud ring at the doorbell.

Bedford jumps to his feet, very excited. He has this goofy look on his face again. "Do not be alarmed, Your Excellency," he tells the Doc. "It is another true friend of the cause."

We hear Wigginton open the front door and say hello to somebody and these footsteps come down the hall. Bedford rushes to the doorway, turns and makes a bow:

"May I present a trusted comrade, Your Excellency?" he says. The Doc nods and Bedford steps to one side. "Operative Graham," he announces in a loud voice.

WELL, OF course I expect to see another goof walk in and you can knock me off the chair with a damp sponge when this little blonde shows in the doorway.

She is about twenty years old with a shape that will put her in front in any company and the first look I get at her I know she is no chump. She gives Bedford a big smile and pats him on the arm as she goes by.

The Doc is on his feet and the blonde marches right up to him and holds out her hand. She looks up into his face with a pair of blue lamps that you could drown a horse in. "I hope you are a friend of Bedford's," she says.

The Doc nods down at her, very solemn. "Believe me, Miss Graham," he tells her, "Bedford has no truer friends at this moment than Colonel Allan and myself." He slips her a slow wink and turns to Bedford. "You have done well in trusting Operative Graham," he says.

The dame smiles at the Doc. "Call me Rosemary," she says. "That is what all my friends call me." She sits down in a big chair and looks up at Bedford. "You are not going out again tonight, are you?"

Bedford stands up straight and stares at the ceiling. "We must not relax our vigilance for one moment," he says. "The enemy is cunning and unscrupulous."

Rosemary looks at the Doc and a big tear about the size of a tennis ball rolls down her cheek. "Please," she says, "won't you make him get some rest?"

The Doc walks over to Bedford. "Operative Sprockle," he says, very crisp, "go to your quarters. Colonel Allan will watch outside the house for the remainder of the night."

I don't go for this. I open my mouth for a squawk when it dawns on me that the Doc is starting the pitch. The Doc is no hand to take charge of anybody unless he can see a percentage in it. I click my heels together and give with a snappy salute.

"Very good, Your Excellency," I tell him.

The Doc gives me a look and I can see he is pleased I catch on so quick. He walks over and pulls a long silk rope hanging by the door. Wigginton comes in so fast I figure he has been glued to the keyhole.

"Mr. Bedford is retiring," the Doc tells him. He pushes the kid into Wigginton's grip and watches the butler steer him up the stairs.

The dame skips across the room and plants a big kiss on the Doc's red face. I get set in case she wishes to include me in this activity but she is too busy being pleased with the Doc.

"You are wonderful," she says. "Poor Bedford hasn't had a decent night's sleep in weeks." She steps back and looks up at him. "Where did you come from? Have you known Bedford long?"

The Doc shakes his head. "We just met the boy a few hours ago," he says. "Mr. Allan and myself were robbed of our automobile and all of our money. We were walking toward Sprockleburg when we encountered Bedford. As a medical man I was interested in his symptoms." He digs into his clothes and comes up with a gold-edged card. "I am Doctor Pierce of New York City."

The dame looks down at the card and then gives the Doc another treatment with the blue eyes. "You were sent by Providence," she says. "Wigginton and I have been so worried about Bedford. If his Uncle Gerstle finds out he has become so..." She stops and another pair of these big tears shows up.

The Doc pats her on the shoulder. "Sit down and tell us all about it," he says.

The dame parks in a chair and dabs at her lamps with a handkerchief. "Bedford is not insane, Doctor Pierce," she tells him. "You must believe that. He is just—well—not grown up."

The Doc takes out his cheaters with the black tie-rope on them and puts them on. "I see," he says. "A case of retarded or arrested development along certain lines. I have encountered many similar problems during my medical career."

Of course I know very well that the only medical career the Doc ever had was when he peddled a couple thousand bottles of snake oil around the carnivals some years back but he is going so good on this pitch I do not even snicker.

The dame brightens up. "Then you can help Bedford?"

"I think so," the Doc tells her. He turns to me. "As a layman of wide experience in this field," he says, "what is your opinion, Mr. Allan?"

Well, I have seen as many crackpots as the next guy and in my book this Bedford is strictly no dice but I pull down my eyebrows and look solemn. "My prognosis is favorable," I tell him.

THE DOC gives me a dirty look. He does not like it when I use these five-dollar words as sometimes I do not put them in the right place. He hauls out his black note-book and a pencil and turns back to the dame. "Tell me all about Bedford," he says. "I must have a complete history."

These big blue eyes are shining like stars. "Where shall I start?" she asks.

"Begin with today and work back," the Doc tells her. "What is Bedford's present situation?"

The dame wrinkles her brow. "Bedford is twenty-two years old," she says. "He came into this portion of his grandfather's estate when he was twenty-one and has lived here alone except for Wigginton ever since. His father and mother died when he was a small child."

The Doc pricks up his ears like he hears a feed-bucket rattling. "Then Bedford manages his own financial affairs?"

"Yes," she says. "His Uncle Gerstle was his guardian until Bedford came of age." She frowns and taps her foot on the carpet. "Gerstle Sprockle is a pompous old windbag and he has made Bedford miserable for years. He tried to retain control of Bedford's stock in the woolen mills and he also has tried to force Bedford to go to work in the mill. Bedford hates the mill," she says. She looks up at the Doc and her eyes are scared. "If Gerstle Sprockle finds out how Bedford has been acting…"

The Doc pats her on the knee. "There, there, Rosemary," he says. "We will not let Uncle Gerstle put Bedford in an institution." He thinks for a minute. "Exactly how much property does Bedford own?"

"He owns this house and five acres of land around it," she tells him. "His income from stock in the mills is about fifteen thousand a year and in addition Bedford has over fifty thousand in cash which he keeps in a safe deposit box in the bank." She turns a bright red and looks the Doc square in the eye. "In other words, Doctor Pierce, Bedford is a good catch."

The Doc pats her on the knee again but I figure he would rather be upstairs patting Bedford on the pocketbook. "I assume that your interest in Bedford is not entirely financial?" he says.

Rosemary shakes her head. "I am in love with him," she says in a low voice. "I have always loved him."

The Doc smiles at her. "Bedford is a lovable young man," he says. He writes in his notebook for a couple of minutes and when he looks up I can see he has the pitch all figured out. "The case is simple," he says. "Bedford is trying to escape from his Uncle Gerstle and a job in the mills by pretending he is a Secret Service agent."

"Yes," the dame says. "That is probably true. Bedford has always been crazy about books and movies dealing with spies and intrigue. A week ago he had an awful row with his uncle. That night he went out and did not return until morning. He told Wigginton that he had been shadowing an enemy spy. Wigginton was worried and told me about it." She shakes her head. "We haven't been able to decide what to do."

The Doc frowns. "I would like to give the boy my personal attention," he says, "but unfortunately we cannot remain here. Mr. Allan and I have just suffered a considerable financial loss and we must hasten back to New York and arrange for a loan from our bankers until some securities we have can be cashed. Perhaps we can return to Sprockleburg in a week or so."

Rosemary jumps up out of the chair. "No, no," she hollers, "you mustn't go away. Next week would be too late." She puts her hand on the Doc's shoulder. "I have some money," she says. "Tell me what your fee will be and I will gladly pay it."

The Doc shakes his head. "I could not accept a fee from you," he says, "but I might consider a small loan, say a thousand dollars, to be repaid after our return to New York."

Rosemary turns on a smile that nearly knocks me out of the chair. "I will get it from the bank in the morning," she tells him. She plants another big kiss on the Doc and skips to the door. "I will sleep well tonight," she says. "I have implicit confidence in you, Doctor Pierce."

I CLIMB into a pair of Bedford's pajamas that Wigginton has put out for me and wrap a big bathrobe around me and go into the Doc's room. He has smuggled a jug of Bedford's bourbon upstairs and he pours me a dose.

"Well," I tell him, "this is a quick score. A grand will send us on our way in good shape."

"I am surprised at you, pony boy," the Doc says. "Surely you do not believe that I would take that nice little girl's money and run out of town with it. It would be unethical."

I take a long swallow of the bourbon. "Look, Doc," I tell him. "I know you are a soft touch for a dame but this place is loaded with dynamite. Uncle Gerstle and a couple of guys with white coats are a cinch to move in on Bedford before long and then where will we be?"

The Doc grins. "We will be a long way from here, pony boy," he says. "And we will have more than a paltry thousand dollars in our pants pockets." He lowers his voice. "Do not forget about that bale of folding money Bedford has in a bank vault," he says. "I have a little plan in mind."

I am usually a sucker for the Doc's little plans but this set-up has me jittery. "Whatever it is, I hope it is quick," I tell him. "I do not approve of lingering here very long."

"It will be quick," the Doc says. "We are going to shock Bedford back to reality. His mind is sound but he is living in a world of fantasy. I believe a severe financial loss will restore him to our midst."

"Well," I tell him, "after the way you frogged it across the road when Belford popped out of those bushes I figure you owe him a shock."

THE NEXT morning after we put on the ham and eggs we gather in the library with Bedford. He has had a good snooze and his eyes are bright and clear. "What are the orders of the day, Your Excellency?" he asks the Doc.

The Doc looks very serious. "We must proceed carefully, Operative Sprockle," he says. "No one must know that Colonel Allan and myself are in the vicinity." He looks up at a clock on the wall. "I have given Operative Rosemary Graham a secret mission to perform to Sprockleburg. When she arrives I wish to see her alone."

Bedford bugs out his eyes. "I trust you have not asked her to exercise her feminine wiles on some enemy agent," he says. "I would not like that."

The Doc frowns at him. "No sacrifice is too great for the cause," he says, "but at present I do not think we will be forced to such extreme measures. The mission is very simple and is related to finances."

Bedford looks at the Doc very hard. "My financial situation is excellent," he says. "I will be proud to furnish whatever funds are necessary."

I begin to get nervous. I am always leery of these pitches that jump up and cuddle in your lap. I flag the Doc to slow down but he pays no attention. He moves over close to Bedford and talks right in his ear.

"We have only known you a short time, Operative Sprockle," he says, "but I am about to entrust you with a secret that is of vital importance to the cause." He glances at me. "Bring down the despatch case, Colonel," he says.

I have a hard time staying under a gallop on this trip to the bedroom and I am shaking like a leaf when I hand the Doc his suitcase. I get into a chair and try to hold still.

The Doc opens the keester and brings out a bunch of papers printed up with red and blue curlycues around the edges. "This is very confidential, Operative Sprockle," he says. "You must not breathe a word of this to anyone, not even Operative Rosemary Graham."

Bedford raises his hand like he is in the dock. "Not a word, Your Excellency," he says, "I swear it."

The Doc riffles the papers onto the table like he is dealing a blackjack hand. "These shares of stock represent control of oil fields that are of immense value to the cause," he says. "Enemy agents have already made three attempts to steal them. Only Colonel Allan's daring and resource saved them from the brigands who robbed us last night." He pulls a fountain pen out of his pocket. "I am going to endorse these securities over to you. You will place them in a safe deposit box in a bank and hold them until I ask for their return." He starts writing on the papers. "I will also notify Mr. Irving Robbins, a good friend of the cause and president of the Hotshot Oil Company, that you are in possession of this stock."

Bedford is so excited he can hardly hold still but he finally gets his signature on the papers and the transfer form the Doc writes out. He stuffs the papers in his pocket and salutes. "Any further orders, Your Excellency?" he asks.

"Yes," the Doc says. "There is another small matter. We need a certain sum of money for a project we have in mind. Not a large sum, only fifty thousand dollars."

Bedford salutes again. "I have that sum available," he says. "I will get it out of the bank when I put these securities in."

The Doc smiles and I can see him relax. I find I am sweating a little although it is a cool day. "That will be fine," the Doc says. He pats Bedford on the shoulder. "These shares of stock will constitute security for the fifty thousand," he says. "They are worth many times that amount."

I know that this is strictly a legitimate transaction as this Irving Robbins is an old pal of the Doc's and he is actually president of this Hotshot outfit although the Hotshot holdings are nothing but a bunch of pasture land down in Oklahoma and the Doc has not even seen Irving Robbins for ten years. We have been lugging this oil stock around for years but we never find a chump that will go for it.

The Doc calls Wigginton in and gets an envelope and an airmail stamp from him as he wishes to get this deal over with. The Doc is a great hand for legal procedure unless it costs us money.

The Doc hands Bedford the letter and sends him off to the village about ten minutes before the little blonde comes in. She has the grand on her in C notes and it is a great relief to me when I see this cash disappear into the Doc's pocket.

THIS ROSEMARY is one of these lucky dames that looks even more tasty in the daytime than she does under soft lights. "How is Bedford this morning, Doctor?" she asks.

The Doc smiles at her. "He is fine," he tells her. "I have given, him a little errand to do in the village." He looks at the dame very serious. "I have worked out a course of treatment that I think will be effective," he tells her. "But I must have an entirely free hand." He walks across the room and pats Rosemary on the shoulder a couple of times. For a minute I wish I have a mop of gray hair and a haybelly so I can go around patting blondes without getting my face slapped. "You are very distracting, my dear," he says, "and Bedford must not be distracted at this stage. I think it will be wise if you remain away from this house for the next week."

Rosemary nods her head up and down. "I will stay away," she says, "but you must promise to let me know how Bedford is getting along."

The Doc takes her by the elbow and steers her to the door. "I will keep you informed of progress," he says, "but you must not expect a miracle. This treatment will take some time."

I get out of my chair and hand Rosemary a low bow as she starts out of the room. I figure this grand she just hands us is deserving of a little courtesy. I am just straightening up when loud footsteps sound in the hall and a short party with a tight black suit and a derby hat marches in. He looks like a cross between a house detective and an undertaker and the minute I lay eyes on him I know he is bad medicine.

The dame backs up and lets out a squeal. "Uncle Gerstle," she says. "What are you doing here?"

Uncle Gerstle walks over to the Doc. "You swindler," he hollers. "What do you mean by selling my nephew fifty thousand dollars worth of wildcat oil stock?" He grabs the telephone off the table. "The bank manager looked over Bedford's shoulder while he was taking out the money and putting the stock in his deposit box," he tells us. "I am going to call the police."

Before I can make a move to interfere with this program Rosemary yanks the phone away from Uncle Gerstle. "You will do nothing of the sort," she says. "Doctor Pierce is a distinguished medical man and Bedford is his patient. Whatever the Doctor has done is part of his treatment."

Uncle Gerstle's fat puss gets very hard and nasty. "So that's it," he hollers. "Just as I suspected, Bedford is a mental case." He marches to the door and turns, giving us all a big piece of a dirty look. "I will have Bedford committed to an asylum the minute I can get hold of a judge tomorrow morning."

THE MINUTE Uncle Gerstle is gone Rosemary turns on the Doc. These big blue eyes are narrowed up so you can hardly see them and she is showing a lot of teeth. "So that is why you wanted me to stay away from this house," she says. "You planned to take Bedford's money and leave town."

It is coming too fast for me and for the first time since I know him the Doc is stopped cold in his tracks. He opens his mouth a couple of times but nothing comes out. I move over close to Rosemary.

"Let us put the slug on this filly," I tell the Doc. "Then we can care for Bedford when he comes and be on our way."

The Doc shakes his head. "You know I do not approve of violence, pony boy," he says. He smiles sadly at the dame. "Do not think too hardly of us, my dear," he says. "I will admit that the treatment we had in mind for Bedford would work out to our financial advantage, but I am still convinced it would have been effective. The loss of a large sum of money through the medium of people so closely associated with this G-man complex of his would have furnished a shock that would restore him to normal."

Rosemary looks him right in the eye. "Do not bother me with any more of your silvery words," she says. She holds out her pink mitt. "I will take my thousand dollars now, and when Bedford arrives you will give me his fifty thousand."

The Doc makes a slow reach for his leather and flutters the lettuce into her hand. "You are a clever girl, Rosemary," he says. He gives her another sad smile. "Please do not disillusion Bedford at this point. It would be very bad for him. Allow us to remain here until tomorrow and I will then break the news of our departure gently as possible to the boy."

Rosemary looks up at him and her lip is shaking. "You are not entirely bad," she says. She turns away and a couple of these tennis balls start down her cheeks. I am practically weeping myself. Especially when she crams the thousand dollars into her handbag and snaps it shut. I cannot stay around to see her take the fifty grand away from Bedford so I head out for the bedroom.

That night the Doc paces the floor while I sit in his room working on the bourbon and laying plans to move out with a couple of these lounge tweeds of Bedford's when we depart next morning. At least I figure on making that much of a score but I do not mention these plans to the Doc as he has some very peculiar ideas about this kind of larceny.

"Well," I tell him, "these little plans of yours do not work out when there is a smart dame around. Although I will have to admit that you handle the dame O.K. in this cause. Uncle Gerstle was the jump you couldn't see when you started to gallop the course."

"I am not through galloping," the Doc says. "We are still in the vicinity of this fifty thousand dollars and we may get a bite at it yet."

WE GATHERED in the library the next morning and the Doc is telling Bedford that we must go away for a short time when Wigginton walks in with this telegram on a silver platter. He takes it over to Rosemary and she tears it open and reads it. She turns to the Doc with a very peculiar look on her peaches-and-cream pan.

"Tell me the truth, Doctor Pierce," she says. "Were you the actual owner of this Hotshot oil stock, and is your transfer of the stock to Bedford a legitimate transaction?"

The Doc nods. "All of my transactions are within the law," he tells her. "I am always careful."

Rosemary snaps her handbag open and pulls out Bedford's roll. She looks up at Wigginton. "You will be a witness," she says. "I am paying Doctor Pierce fifty thousand dollars for the Hotshot oil stock he has already transferred to Bedford."

Wigginton nods. "I understand," he says. "I am a witness."

The Doc looks at the dough in his hand and then he looks at Rosemary. He looks sick. "So the field came in," he says, very soft.

Rosemary laughs and throws him the telegram. The Doc takes one look at it and passes it to me. It takes me a minute to get it but then I am sick too. It says:

HAVE BEEN TRYING TO LOCATE YOU FOR MONTHS HOTSHOT HAS THIRTY GUSHERS YOUR STOCK WORTH A MILLION DO NOT COMPLETE SALE IF YOU CAN HELP IT.
                              IRVING ROBBINS.

The train is pulling out of Sprockleburg before I say anything to the Doc. I have been concentrating on how pleasant it would be to have a million dollars.

"Well," I tell him. "Your treatment did not work on Bedford. The last thing he tells me before we leave is that he has his eye on a couple of fresh enemy agents that he plans to shadow. I doubt if Bedford ever comes back to normal."

The Doc shakes his head. "Sometimes I think you are not quite bright, pony boy," he says. "According to the record, Bedford is the financial brains of the Sprockle family. He is now in a position to be thoroughly eccentric.

He has a million dollars and a beautiful blonde. It takes a smart guy to make a score like that." He pats himself on the wallet that is bulging the front of his swayback coat. "However, I should say that fifty thousand dollars was a most reasonable fee for my particular brand of medical attention in this case."

I take a feel of my own fat leather. "Sure," I tell him. "And it was also strictly ethical."

PAINLESS OPERATION

"I FAIL TO UNDERSTAND HOW
YOU CLASSIFY MR. WARBURTON
AS A THIEF," THE DOC TELLS ME.
"HE IS A PROSPEROUS BUSINESS
MAN." PROSPEROUS IS RIGHT,
I'M THINKING. A GUY SHOULD
BE WHEN HE MAKES HIS OWN
LETTUCE AND WARBURTON
DIDN'T GET THE NAME OF "WARM
WAMPUM WILBUR" FROM SELLING
APPLES.

THE **MEETING** has been on about a week and the bar in the clubhouse is doing all right. The Doc has his back to me but I spot him by his wide black skimmer and swayback coat. I start toward him but I haul up short when I notice he is talking to Warm Wilbur.

Warm Wilbur is a party about my age with a fat face and a carnation in his buttonhole. He has been around for some time but I never have any truck with him if I can help it.

The Doc happens to turn his head and I am somewhat surprised when he gives me the office not to move in.

For once I don't pay any attention to him. I squeeze in beside Warm Wilbur and give him a poke in the ribs. "How is the hot stuff moving these days?" I ask him.

Wilbur gives me a sour look. "Go away," he says. "I am busy."

"From what I hear," I tell him. "You are always busy."

Warm Wilbur turns to the Doc. "This guy is named Allan, Doctor Pierce," he says. "He is nothing but a common hustler around the racetracks and I would advise you to give him plenty of room."

The Doc glares at me. He is mad because I disregard his signal. "I have heard tales of such low characters," he says. "The authorities should remove them from circulation."

I get a grin out of the Doc, but I can't let Wilbur get by with this. "Keep a civil tongue in your head," I tell him. "Or somebody will yank it out and slap down your big ears."

Wilbur smiles at me quick. "It was all in fun, chum," he says. "Let me buy you a drink."

"Thanks, sweetheart," I tell him. "I am not thirsty."

THE DOC is still mad when I drop into his room that night. "I expected you a week ago, pony boy," he says, scowling at me. "And in the future I will thank you to keep your hands out of my pitches unless you are invited in."

I just laugh at him. "O.K., Doc," I tell him. "But from what I see this afternoon you are due to finish a bad second in this little parlay."

The Doc cools out quick. "There is a jug of bourbon in my suitcase," he says. "Let us relax while you describe how I am running behind."

I pour a couple of big doses, pull off my shoes and stretch on the bed. "Look, Doc," I tell him. "You are the smartest operator I know in your line, but you should never go near a racetrack unless I am there to steer you around. You have fallen among thieves."

The Doc's big red face is serious. "I suppose you refer to my friend Mr. Warburton," he says. "I fail to understand how you classify him as a thief. He is a prosperous business man on a vacation. We have been whiling away the time wagering against each other on the races."

"Tell me how you and Warm Wilbur while away the time," I ask him.

"As you know, I am a great believer in the power of a percentage," the Doc says. "I encountered Mr. Warburton in the bar on opening day. We had each sustained minor

The Doc smiles like this Pinkerton
has asked him to have a mint julep.

losses on the first race and while we were condoling one
another a little plan occurred to me.

"I have observed that about half of the races have an odd
number of horses in them, say eleven or fifteen. I suggested
to Mr. Warburton that we wager equal sums against each
other—one of us to take the odd-numbered horses, the
other the even numbers. Strangely enough I happen to
win each time and of course I choose the odd-numbers."

I have to laugh. "I get it. With eleven ponies in a race
the odd numbers have six chances at a win, the even only
five." I don't have to ask how he always wins the cut. The
Doc is no raw hand around a deck of cards.

"Exactly," the Doc says. "At Mr. Warburton's suggestion
we appointed one of the bartenders, a gentleman named

Kelly, as stakeholder. I always tip Mr. Kelly handsomely when I win and we are firm friends."

THIS IS what I have been waiting for.

"Take a firm grip on the bourbon, Doc," I tell him. "I am about to relate some unpleasant facts about your profits, Warm Wilbur Warburton, and your firm friend Mr. Kelly."

The Doc is paying close attention. "Shoot," he says.

"To begin with," I tell him, "Your friend Warburton is a business man but he will never get a vacation unless the G-men send him up the country. He is always busy and he makes good money. In fact it takes an expert to tell it from the kind that Uncle Sam puts out. Wilbur is known in certain circles as Warm Wampum Wilbur."

The Doc jumps to his feet and lets out the worst string of bad words I ever listened to. "Warm Wampum," he hollers. "A counterfeiter!"

"That's right," I tell him rubbing it in a little.

The Doc scowls. "But how does he work the switch?"

"This bartender, Kelly," I tell him. "This firm friend of yours, Cough-Drop Kelly. He is the reason I leave this afternoon when Wilbur offers to buy me a drink. I am afraid Cough-Drop will serve me one of his specials. He is called Cough Drop because when a party takes a swallow of one of his specials he coughs and then drops flat on the floor."

The Doc waves his hand. "Spare me the horrid details," he says. He thinks for a minute and then pulls out a leather about three inches thick and shakes a bunch of cabbage on the bed. "Can you distinguish Mr. Warburton's merchandise?"

I sort the bills into two piles. They are mostly hundreds and fifties. Only three of the fifties will get by a smart house man. I show him where the background on the pictures is too white and how Wilbur uses a sharp blue instead of green in some spots.

The Doc shakes his head sadly. "My own vanity has contributed to my downfall." He stands looking at the piles of bills on the bed. "It is a clever play," he says. "Kelly puts my good money in one pocket and pays me out of the other. I suppose the sensible thing would be to ditch these sizzling simoleons and write it off the book, but I cannot accept defeat so easily. There must be an answer somewhere."

"Well," I tell him. "I have never liked Wilbur and I thoroughly disapprove of Cough-Drop and his specials. If you can think up a little plan I will be glad to go along."

The Doc snaps his fingers. "I think I have a faint glimmering," he says. "You rustle the town and see what you can learn of Mr. Warburton's private affairs. We must leave no stone unturned."

"O.K.," I tell him. "I will track Wilbur to his lair."

WARM WILBUR is not hard to overtake. He is in the biggest clip joint in the town. Wilbur is a short guy with a dollar and I cannot figure him going for the prices in this place until I see who is with him. He is pushing a dame around the floor by the name of Theodora Dibble. I am not surprised to see Wilbur taking dead aim at Theodora although she packs about thirty pounds in the wrong spots, has a voice that will scare a hog out of its growth, and is legged up like the top section of a quarter-pole.

Theodora is a bargain because she is the only get of an old appleknocker by the name of J. Harrison Dibble. This J. Harrison owns a bunch of farms up the state and also has a piece of three or four banks. The odds are six, two and even that Theodora will harvest a big bale of folding money when old J. Harrison hangs up his tack.

As it happens old J. Harrison is quite a pal of mine. This comes about right after he crawls down out of the hills and starts to buy racehorses. A couple of gyps are trying to hang a broken-down plater on him and one day I am leaning up against J. Harrison at the rail and he asks me what I think of this plater he is considering buying.

I tell him the track vet plans to put this beetle in a museum when he finally falls over as he has everything wrong with him that can happen to a horse. At the same time I put in a couple of boosts for a three-year-old called Greased Heels which a friend of mine is anxious to unload at this point.

Well, J. Harrison takes my advice and buys Greased Heels and it turns out very well.

In fact it turns out that all Greased Heels needs is a few square meals as he wins a good stake about a month after he lands in J. Harrison Dibble's barn. J. Harrison takes me out that night and buys me a big dinner with a lot of wine and he also tells me that if I ever need a favor to call on him.

I think about this as I sit in the corner and watch Wilbur and Theodora bumping and bouncing around the floor. Suddenly a little guy walks up behind Wilbur and taps him on the shoulder. I recognize this little guy as a jockey named A. Goold who is contract rider for Theodora's old man.

Wilbur seems pleased to see this little guy, which is not very surprising, but it puzzles me a little when I notice that Theodora also seems pleased. This A. Goold is just about the ugliest jock I ever see.

A. Goold puts his arm around Theodora as far as he can and as he is fresh and lively Theodora yanks him around the

floor at a good clip. She does a lot of laughing and hollering down at A. Goold. I can see this is going on for some
time and I figure I have enough information anyhow so I
march myself back to the hotel.

THE DOC pays close attention when I describe this
scene to him. "What kind of a lad is this jockey, Goold?"
he asks me.

"Well," I tell him, "he wins some good races for J. Harrison in the last couple of years, but lately I hear that he
learns there are nice sums to be made by strong boys who
will hold a horse down at a time when certain parties might
not want him to win."

The Doc nods. "I will keep that in mind." He thinks for
a minute. "Do you think this Goold is a serious rival for
Theodora's affections?"

"I give up figuring those angles years ago," I tell him.
"Wilbur is no bargain for type but he is ten lengths better
than A. Goold. However, Theodora is in no shape to pick
and choose."

"Well," the Doc says. "Perhaps it will fit in somewhere."

The next morning I am moping around the stables when
I run into J. Harrison Dibble. He takes me right into his
tackroom and breaks out a jug. "This is an occasion," he
says. "I shall always be grateful to you for advising me to
purchase Greased Heels. He is a fine colt and will win the
stake tomorrow."

"How about this New York horse, Rollaway?" I ask him.

"Rollaway is a good horse," he says. "But my colt is at the
top of his form. His works have been sensational."

"O.K.," I tell him. "I will send in a few shekels on the
front end of the Heels tomorrow."

J. Harrison closes the door and lowers his voice. "You gave me some good advice on one occasion, Mr. Allan," he says. "I have a difficult personal problem and it just occurred to me that you might be able to help."

"Well," I tell him. "I am no Dorothy Dix, but I will do what I can."

"I am sure of that," he says. He gets a funny look on his brown old face, takes a swallow of the drink in his hand. "It concerns my daughter, Theodora," he says. "She has reached the age where she is thinking seriously of love and marriage."

"Perhaps some low character is trying to take advantage of her youth and innocence?"

"That is the situation exactly," he tells me. "But there are two low characters involved."

It is coming pretty fast but I give him another boost. "I see Theodora in a trap last night dancing with Wilbur Warburton and this jockey," I tell him. "Wilbur has a bad reputation, although it has never been proved in court, but I figure A. Goold is an honest workingman. Maybe you do not want Theodora to hook up with an employee?"

J. Harrison shakes his head. "I am not a snob," he says. "But between you and me this A. Goold is a little crook. I am certain he has pulled my horses on many occasions."

I figure it is time to go. "Well," I tell him. "I do not have much experience in such matters but I will think it over. I would hate to see a charming girl like Theodora in the clutches of either of these characters."

J. Harrison smiles and pumps my hand. "Forgive me for burdening you with my domestic difficulties," he says. "Drop in anytime, Mr. Allen. I am always glad to see you."

I go back to town and have lunch with the Doc in his room. He listens carefully while I tell him about my talk with J. Harrison. "That situation is very interesting," he says. "But I think I have a quick solution to Wilbur. I do not wish to arouse his suspicions, so I will play along with him on the first race. Station yourself near us at the bar and when I leave for a moment you move in and keep him in conversation until I get back. I will do the rest."

"O.K.," I tell him. "I will keep Wilbur busy, but if there is a beef, watch out for Cough-Drop Kelly. He is a very rough customer."

The Doc grins. "There will be no beef. The operation will be painless."

THE OPERATION takes very little time. The numbers are hardly on the board from the first race when the Doc tows Wilbur into the bar. He takes a spot a few yards from me and smiles at Wilbur.

"I hate to take your money so often, Mr. Warburton," he says, "but don't worry—you will probably win the next seven races."

He glances at me and raises his voice a little. "You must excuse me while I make a brief trip to the comfort station," he says.

I have said hardly a dozen words to Wilbur and he is just getting good and mad at me when the Doc returns. I slide away and watch carefully while the Doc straightens up the rose in Wilbur's lapel. His getaway is smooth, too.

"An old digestive ailment is troubling me," he tells Wilbur. "I must hasten into town and contact a reliable pharmacist immediately."

The Doc has to make this phone call on the way out and I wait at the gate for him. He comes up rubbing his hands. "A neat, tidy job," he says, gloatingly. "With no loose ends."

"That dip was a neat job," I tell him. "I see some two-fingered artists in my time but nobody ever lifts a leather with less fuss and bother."

The Doc grins. "It is many years since I snatched a poke," he says. "And of course I would not do such a thing except in a dire emergency. It is against the law. But it is nice to know I have not lost my touch."

"Are we all squared away with Wilbur now?" I ask him.

The Doc frowns. "Unfortunately he was carrying a trifle over five thousand in his wallet. I have about two grand left over as I did not want to over-pay him. He might get suspicious."

"Wilbur was born suspicious," I tell him. "You had better slide the rest of that warm wampum down a sewer." I have to laugh. "I wish we could be there when the Pinkertons put the arm on Wilbur and Cough-Drop. Especially when Wilbur sees his own merchandise staring him in the face."

The Doc chuckles. "That will be a pleasant moment," he says. He shakes his head. "I hate to throw this merchandise away. Maybe we can think of a good use for it."

"Sure," I tell him. "Maybe we can rig a snappy crap game with a couple of blind guys."

I AM a little nervous when I think this over the next morning as I know Wilbur has a few friends around and I figure maybe he will tumble to this dodge the Doc puts over. I try to get the Doc to leave town suddenly but he just laughs at me.

"I would not miss seeing this stake race for anything," he says. "And I think Wilbur will be busy conferring with the G-men for some time. Furthermore I am anxious to meet your friend, J. Harrison Dibble. He sounds like a handy man to know."

The Doc is very fond of people with a lot of dollars. "O.K.," I tell him. "I will put you away with J. Harrison and we will watch the stake, but let us then leave town. I just remember that Cough-Drop Kelly has some friends in the vicinity, too."

The Doc and J. Harrison take to each other right off and I leave them gabbing away at a good clip while I take a mope around the stables to see what is doing in the stake. I get talking to a bookie by the name of Chicago Charlie and he tells me a strange thing.

"A bunch of fresh dough comes into town this morning," he says, "and they are sending it in on Rollaway. Greased Heels is now three-to-two and getting better fast."

I mention this to the Doc when he comes along and he is interested. "That's fine," he says. "We will take a ride on Greased Heels, just to pass the time, of course."

"You do not understand these things, Doc," I tell him. "When fresh dough shows up like this it is always smart dough. The smart way to bet is along with it."

He shakes his head. "I had a nice chat with Mr. Dibble," he says. "And he introduced me to his jockey, A. Goold. Both of them assured me that Greased Heels will win."

"If J. Harrison is in shape to ride the horse himself, I will believe it," I tell him. "But I will not trust this A. Goold anywhere, especially in a saddle."

The Doc shakes his head. "I have a feeling A. Goold will do his best today," he says.

Well, I know that if A. Goold does his best Greased Heels will run off and hide from Rolloway. I watch the Doc send a couple of grand along on Greased Heels, and finally I shut my eyes and slap in a grand.

The race is a shoo-in. A. Goold and Greased Heels set sail from the gate and they never look back except when Greased Heels turns and gives Rollaway the old horse-cackle as he slides under the finish-wire.

While we are stuffing the cabbage into our wallets at the pay-off booth, the Doc says: "I have a phone call to make and then I think we should hurry out of town."

We go out into the main room of the clubhouse and the Doc has his hand on the telephone when I notice these two big guys coming toward us.

THE CLUBHOUSE is crowded and anyhow the Doc is not legged up for a quick start so all we can do is hold still. The biggest guy shows the Doc what he has under his coat and the other one clamps my arm.

"The manager of the track would like to speak to you gentlemen," the big one says.

The Doc smiles like this Pinkerton has asked him to have a mint julep. "Certainly," he says. "We are always glad to cooperate with the law."

It suddenly is a chilly day. By the time we make the manager's office I am throwing a cold sweat.

The track manager is polite. "We have information that a gang of counterfeiters is operating in the vicinity," he says. "Would you object to showing us your money so that we may ascertain if you have been victimized?"

The Doc yanks out his leather and tosses it on the desk. He holds his arms out from his side. "Perhaps you would like to search me?"

Well, I have seen some shakes in my time but by the time these Pinkertons get through with us we have no secrets. When we are back in our clothes the biggest Pinkerton holds out his hand to the Doc. "No hard feelings, I hope," he says, friendly-like.

The Doc grins at him. "Not at all," he says. "I admire your diligence and devotion to duty."

The minute we are outside the Doc heads for the phone booth again. I grab the arm.

"Listen," I tell him. "Let's forget this telephone and let us get back to the hotel and ditch that hot dough before these Pinkertons think of searching your room. They had more than a dim suspicion."

The Doc nods. "I agree with you," he says. "But that money is not in my room. This phone call will attend to its final disposition."

I am burning up but he won't say a word until we get back to the hotel. "It is time to go and we must move fast," he says. "I will meet you on the train very shortly."

We have about fifty miles behind us when the Doc drops into my seat. "I told you that I had a little private chat with A. Goold," he says. "A. Goold is not very bright and it did not take me long to extract an admission from him that he was to be paid for retarding the progress of Greased Heels in favor of this horse Rollaway. The rascals who corrupted him had agreed to pay him the paltry sum of one thousand dollars for his efforts. When I offered him double that in cash he readily agreed to do the honest thing by Greased Heels."

It takes a minute to sink in. "You bribed A. Goold with Wilbur's two thousand in warm wampum?" I get the rest of it. "And that phone call you just made before was another tip-off to the police?"

The Doc grins. "That will be a touching reunion when A. Goold joins Mr. Warburton and Mr. Kelly in jail."

I have to laugh. "That also fixes up J. Harrison and his domestic problem very nicely."

The Doc chuckles. "I think Mr. Dibble's gratitude may pay off some day." He gets up. "I hear the climate in California is very healthful this time of year. I think I will attend the fall meeting at Bay Meadows."

I grin at him. "Watch your step around the ponies, Doc. And don't take any wooden nickels."

THE DOCTOR'S TREATMENT

"THE DOC ALMOST LOSES INTEREST IN GOLDBERG O'TOOLE WHEN HE HEARS HE IS OUT OF FUNDS. BUT THE FACT THAT THIS APPLEKNOCKER OWNS 6,000 ACRES OF RICH COTTON LAND PUTS A DIFFERENT LIGHT ON THE MATTER—A $10,000 LIGHT!"

WE ARE standing on the deck of this tub watching the roustabouts hustle the freight aboard. I am not feeling too good. The ponies give us a bad time the last couple days of the meeting and this is the only transportation we can afford. I am trying to decide which smells worse, the river or this old tub, when the Doc pokes me.

"I see we are to have company on this delightful voyage," he says.

A little guy with a wrinkled white suit and no hat on is trotting up the gangway. He has a round pink face with big blue eyes and a shock of curly blond hair sticking up off his head. A big guy is pushing a wheelbarrow along behind him and when I realize what is on this wheelbarrow I have to laugh. Before I can say anything to the Doc the little guy is beside us.

"Why, Mr. Allan," he says. "What are you doing here?"

"Well," I tell him, "if this scow holds together, we are taking a ride up the river."

I wink at the Doc. "This is Goldberg O'Toole, Doctor Pierce. Goldberg is a great inventor."

The Doc parts his swayback coat so his white vest shows and sticks out his big mitt. "I am delighted to meet a fellow scientist, Mr. O'Toole," he says. "In my youth I was much interested in mechanical contrivances."

Of course I know very well that the nearest the Doc ever gets to a mechanical contrivance in his youth is when he runs a shell game behind the merry-go-round at the County Fair but the kid swallows it right down.

"My correct name is Robert Emmett O'Toole," he tells the Doc. "The boys around the racetrack refer to me as Goldberg because my invention reminds them of the creations of Rube Goldberg, the comic cartoonist." He points at the bunch of gears and pulleys on the wheelbarrow and smiles. "You may notice a slight resemblance."

I have seen Goldberg's gadget many times in the past month but as the Doc never hangs around the stable area it is his first peek at the Horseman's Handy Helper. He takes out his cheaters with the black ribbon on them and takes a good gander at it.

"A most interesting mechanism," he says.

THIS HORSEMAN'S Helper is about a yard long and two yards high. Besides these gears and pulleys it has about a dozen long flexible pipes sticking up with brushes and suction cups on the ends. Goldberg claims this gadget will cuff off a horse, soap a saddle, wash a blanket and do many other stable chores in jig-time if it is handled properly.

The trouble is nobody ever handles it right, not even Goldberg. In fact the first time he tries to groom a horse with it, the Horseman's Helper acts like it wants to wash a blanket and scares the pony and the guy that owns him half to death.

Goldberg shakes his head at the Doc. "Very few people have displayed interest in my invention," he says. "I must

As Crunchway turns his head, two of the long pipes swing forward and a suction cup clamps on his right ear.

admit defeat. I am completely out of funds and there is nothing to do but go home."

Of course when the Doc hears this he loses interest in Goldberg. The Doc does not hang around people who are out of funds. He wanders up to the front end of the boat and a couple of minutes later I see him talking with the captain.

Goldberg lets out a big sigh. "I suppose I am foolish to take that silly invention home with me," he says. "I should drop it in the river and forget it." He gives me a little smile. "At least I furnished amusement for the boys around the stables."

For some reason I do not feel like laughing at Goldberg O'Toole right now. "You just made a bad start," I tell him. "From what I hear even this guy Edison gets left flat-footed at the post his first couple of times out."

"I shall never be another Thomas Edison," Goldberg says.

I can't give him an argument on this. "How do you happen to build this gadget?" I ask him. "Do your folks own horses?"

"We used to keep a few saddlers," he says, "but now all we have is mules. I live on a cotton plantation and my original intention was to build a mechanical cotton-picker."

"A gadget that picks cotton should do all right in these parts," I tell him.

"The Rust brothers have produced a machine that is far superior to mine," he says. "As a desperate gamble I converted my cotton picker into the Horseman's Helper."

"Maybe you can teach it to pitch hay or pull stumps," I tell him. "The way I figure it these appleknockers can always use one more gadget."

Goldberg just sighs again and shakes his head. I figure we will both bust out crying in a minute so I walk away fast.

It is time to unhitch the boat and start up the river. The captain stops talking to the Doc and begins running up and down the deck, yelling at the hands. The Doc comes over to me.

"This captain is a most interesting personality," he says.

"I am surprised to hear this," I tell him. "In my book he is just another fat Cajun with greasy whiskers and a garlic breath. He could also use a bath."

The Doc grins. "I admit that he is lacking in certain social graces," he says. "But our captain is sound at the core.

He is most unhappy on the river and is saving up his wages so he can buy a cozy little farm."

"This is indeed interesting," I tell him. "I trust he keeps these savings in a handy place."

"That is what I intend to find out," the Doc says. He lowers his voice. "I shall depend on you to keep this O'Toole character out from underfoot."

"O.K.," I tell him. "I will listen to Goldberg's sad tale while you put the shake on the captain."

IT IS a slow trip. We are bucking the current and this tub also stops about every ten miles to throw hunks of cargo to the yokels that live along the bank. The Doc spends most of his time up in the wheelhouse with the captain but from what I hear he is not moving any faster than the boat. I drop into his cabin the second evening and he is reading some hayshaker magazine the captain lends him. He grins at me.

"I shall be an authority on agricultural subjects by the time this voyage is over," he says.

"Well," I tell him, "I hope you plow up this captain's bankroll pretty quick. I am getting bored with this old scow."

I am also getting bored with Goldberg O'Toole. He is a nice little guy but he figures he is the only party in the world who ever has a tough break.

The next morning he starts a sad tale right after breakfast. I pull him up short. "Look," I tell him, "I am a few years older than you are and I am short of shekels most of my life but I do not talk about it unless I am making a touch. You are not the only party around here who is flat broke and you have a home and a family to back up on."

Goldberg shakes his head. "The only family I have is my young sister, Sharon," he says. "Sharon is a lovely girl. She is just twenty-one and I am worried about her future. In less than three months the bank will foreclose the mortgage on our plantation and we will have no home."

"Well," I tell him, "if your sister is a good looking dame you should get her out under the bright lights where she can nudge up against a few parties with dollars in their wallets. There is no percentage in this backwoods set-up."

Goldberg nods. "We would like nothing better," he says. "Neither of us is fond of farming, but it is hard to give up six thousand acres of the finest land along the river to a man like Jeff Crunchway."

"Where does this Crunchway cut in?" I ask him.

"He is president of the local bank and he also owns most of the stock," Goldberg tells me. "Jeff persuaded my father to mortgage the land and invest the proceeds in worthless oil stock. The shock of this loss brought on my father's death. The cotton market has been bad for years and we have not been able to pay off a single dollar." He puts his hand on my shoulder. "I am sorry to have burdened you with my troubles, Mr. Allan," he says. "But it's a long time since I have had a sympathetic listener."

"Well," I tell him, "you are healthy and you have a good line of gab. All you need is to find a racket. You can even go to work, although personally, I will never consider taking such a step."

Goldberg smiles. "Yes, I suppose we will not starve." He thinks for a minute. "Why don't you and Doctor Pierce stop over for a few days? My sister would be delighted to meet you."

"I would be delighted to meet your sister," I tell him. "But Doctor Pierce is engaged in a little problem of research that requires his presence on this boat. I do not think he will consider interrupting his studies at this point."

THAT EVENING the Doc is off his feed. He sits at the table with a blank look on his red face and pays little attention to the rations. I mope into his cabin after dinner and he is sitting on his bunk looking sad.

"The old man has lost his touch, pony boy," he says. "He is ready for the boneyard."

I reach into his suitcase for the bourbon and pour a big dose. He gulps it down but he still looks sad.

"This captain," he says. "I judge him to be a solid citizen. One of nature's noblemen. Now I learn that he is nothing but a common prevaricator. He is also a drunkard." The Doc takes another helping of bourbon and picks up one of these hayshaker magazines the captain lends him off the table. "And to think I spent hours reading this rural rubbish so I could ingratiate myself with that rascal."

I catch on. "The captain has no savings?"

The Doc snorts. "He confessed to me this afternoon that he spends every penny he gets in low grog-shops along the waterfront. That drivel about buying a farm is the vaporings of an alcoholic." He shakes his head. "We must leave this boat at the first opportunity. I cannot bear the sight of that whiskered wastrel."

"Well," I tell him, "Goldberg tells me we arrive at his home town, Riverbend, tomorrow morning. He wishes us to be his guests for a few days at the family plantation."

"Plantation?" the Doc says. He brightens up. "Then this O'Toole family is wealthy?"

"They are flat broke," I tell him. "Also they are getting heaved out of the homestead in a couple of months." I give him a quick run-down on the O'Toole family set-up.

The Doc jumps up and starts walking the stall. "Six thousand acres," he says. "Why, this is an outrage. Those innocent children. Evicted from their home by a heartless, money-grubbing banker."

"Save the spiel for the suckers," I tell him. "What do you have in mind?"

The Doc grins. "Just the vague beginnings of a little plan," he says. He is still holding this hayshaker magazine in his hand. He glances down at it and his eyes open wide. He chuckles. "I think I have it."

I grab the magazine and take a gander at the cover. All I can see is a picture of some big dam the government is putting up out west so the appleknockers in the vicinity will not dry up and blow away. It doesn't make sense but I know better than to ask the Doc any questions. The Doc figures I function better in a caper if I don't know too much about it.

"Get O'Toole in here," the Doc says, very snappy.

I sit around for the next couple of hours while the Doc pumps Goldberg. About all he gets that I have not heard before is that the mortgage is for two hundred thousand and that good cotton land sells for from forty to a hundred dollars an acre.

The Doc figures for a minute. "Why," he says, "you have an equity in this land that must be worth at least fifty thousand dollars."

Goldberg shakes his head. "We would be glad to take half of that," he says. "But there are no buyers for cotton land. And Jefferson Crunchway is a powerful man. He is smart and unscrupulous. He would find some way to block any sale we tried to make."

"I am pleased to hear this," the Doc says. "I like to deal with people of intelligence, especially if they have a streak of larceny in their makeup." He smiles at Goldberg. "I have a plan in mind, a little treatment for Mr. Crunchway. In case we are successful, Mr. Allan and I will expect a portion of the profits—say ten per cent. Is that agreeable?"

Goldberg's pink face is solemn. "I trust your judgment, Doctor Pierce," he says. "I am sure my sister will cooperate."

"Excellent," the Doc says. "I will have a few simple instructions for you in the morning."

SHARON O'TOOLE is waiting at the dock. I am peeking out of the porthole of my cabin as the Doc does not wish the citizens of Riverbend to know we are teamed up with Goldberg. Sharon is a slim blonde with the kind of complexion you can eat with a spoon. She is wearing a blue shirt and a pair of jodhpur riding breeches but I have no trouble deciding she is a dame.

She is standing beside a pair of mules hooked up to a rickety old wagon and when she spots Goldberg she takes a big hug at him. I can see she is very fond of Goldberg. A couple of roustabouts load the Horseman's Helper into the wagon and Sharon and Goldberg rattle off down the road. The Doc is standing behind me.

"Well," I tell him, "I will gladly take a small share in that blonde as my percentage in this deal."

The Doc shakes his head. "We have a busy day before us. We must keep our eyes on the ball." He is wearing his best striped pants and a fresh white vest and he has dusted off his black skimmer and his swayback coat so I figure we will go into action right away. He picks up his suitcase. "We must register at the hotel for the sake of appearances," he tells me.

This Riverbend is by no means a lively burg. Most of the buildings are about a hundred years old and lean up against each other like a bunch of drunks. It is ten o'clock in the morning but nobody is on the main stem but a couple of hound dogs and maybe a dozen pickaninnies.

The hotel proprietor is a dried-up job about ten years older than the town and when the Doc asks him a couple of questions he acts like we are Yankee spies. The Doc always carries a flask of bourbon on his hip for these emergencies and after the proprietor gets a couple of doses down he turns out to be quite a gabby old guy.

He gives the Doc a quick run-down on the location of various plantations in the neighborhood and I notice the Doc copies it all down in his black notebook. The Doc slaps the proprietor on the back and snags the flask when it jars loose.

"Many thanks, friend," he says. He starts the flask toward his hip but the proprietor takes a bob at it like he is ducking for an apple in a washtub, so the Doc slips him one more gurgle. "By the way," he says, "when does the next boat stop in Riverbend?"

The proprietor wipes his chin. "Eight o'clock this evening," he says. "The *Golden Belle*. Fastest boat on the river."

The Doc grins at me. "The breaks are with us, pony boy."

THE FIRST look I get at this banker, Jefferson Crunchway, I figure he is no soft touch. He is about the same age as the Doc, maybe fifty, and he has a square chin and a pair of pale blue eyes that can double for ice cubes. He sits behind his shiny desk and stares at the gold-edged card the Doc slips him.

"I see you are connected with our national government, Doctor Pierce," he says.

The Doc reaches over and clips the card out of Crunch-way's mitt. "How stupid of me," he says. "That is one of my old cards." He tears the pasteboard into little pieces and drops them into the wastebasket. He nods at me. "Until a few weeks ago, Doctor Allan and I were employed as research scientists by the Department of Agriculture. We resigned our positions for a certain reason." He leans forward and drops his voice. "That reason, Mr. Crunchway, brings us to Riverbend."

I sit up straight and try to look like I am a research scientist. I am not surprised when the Doc flashes this card. The Doc has a collection of business cards to fit every occasion.

Crunchway raises a pair of eyebrows that look like they were clipped off a crow. "And this reason?"

The Doc smooths out his face. "We resigned our positions because we saw an opportunity to make a large sum of money. We need this money to equip a laboratory for certain studies we have in mind that will be of great benefit to mankind." He shakes his head. "Unfortunately we are but simple scientists. It did not occur to us that others might see this same opportunity." He lowers his voice. "Those others, Mr. Crunchway, are passengers aboard the *Golden Belle*. They will be in Riverbend at eight o'clock tonight."

Crunchway does not even feel the hook. His voice is excited. "This opportunity is here? In Riverbend?"

The Doc sighs. "We had hoped to handle this ourselves," he says, "but we lack the business experience, and, to put it bluntly, the funds to consummate this enterprise in the short time remaining." He pulls out his black notebook and fixes his cheaters on his nose. "You have a reputation as a man of keen sagacity in business affairs. You are also in a peculiarly favorable position so far as this enterprise is concerned."

Crunchway likes it. He leans back in his chair. "And just what is my position?"

The Doc reads from his notebook. "This bank, which you control, holds a mortgage in the amount of two hundred thousand dollars against six thousand acres of land in the possession of Robert Emmett O'Toole and his sister, Sharon Carroll O'Toole. Is that correct?"

Crunchway nods. "That is correct." The Doc closes the notebook. "The O'Toole mortgage becomes due and payable in exactly eighty-three days." He leans over the desk. "Mr. Crunchway, we must obtain clear title to the O'Toole plantation before the *Golden Belle* docks tonight."

Crunchway looks puzzled. "But that is cotton land. The market is low. The land is worth little more than the amount of the mortgage."

The Doc leans a little closer. "The Department of Agriculture is undertaking an immense project, the nature of which I cannot reveal at this time. Six hundred thousand dollars has been appropriated for the purchase of the O'Toole plantation. It is the only land on the river that will serve this particular purpose."

Crunchway narrows his eyes and I can almost hear the wheels go round. "And these people arriving on the *Golden Belle* also have this information?"

The Doc nods. "They are unscrupulous financiers," he says. "Money-grubbers of the worst type. They are prepared to pay the O'Tooles one hundred thousand dollars for their equity. Then they intend to pay off the mortgage and reap a profit of three hundred thousand dollars."

Crunchway gulps the bait. "We must forestall these villains," he says. He pulls down these eyebrows again. "I suppose you gentlemen have a figure in mind for your share in the proceeds?"

The Doc smiles. "Doctor Allan and I will leave that up to your sense of fair play," he says. "After all, you will probably have to pay the O'Tooles a large sum for their equity."

Crunchway rubs his hands together. "I will have title to the O'Toole plantation before the sun sets," he says. He holds out his mitt. "A gentlemen's agreement. We will share equally in the profits, after all necessary expenditures have been deducted."

The Doc pumps his mitt up and down. He passes it over to me. "A gentlemen's agreement," he says.

WE MAKE it to the hotel in ten seconds flat. The Doc rents the proprietor's flivver and asks him which way is the O'Toole plantation. I am nervous and the fact that this flivver will not do over twelve miles an hour makes me feel no better. When we turn up the driveway I am hand-riding this jalopy like it is in the stretch at Churchill Downs.

The Doc is feeling the pressure, too. Goldberg and Sharon are standing on the porch when we rattle up but the Doc is not polite. "Get this monstrosity out of sight," he says. He hops out. "Come in the house through the back door. That money-grubber will be here any minute."

I drive the flivver into a shed behind the house. I have to grin when I see the Horseman's Helper is also parked in this shed.

It is at least two furlongs from the kitchen door of the O'Toole mansion to the big room in front where the Doc is slipping the low-down to Goldberg and his sister. Sharon is even tastier at close range and for a couple of minutes I even forget Crunchway.

Goldberg is standing beside the window. All of a sudden he lets out a yelp. "He is coming up the drive!"

Sharon turns very pale and the Doc pats her on the shoulder. "Your troubles will soon be over." He smiles at Goldberg. "Be firm, my boy."

Goldberg is pale too. But his eyes are bright and steady. "I will make that scoundrel crawl," he says.

CRUNCHWAY STARTS out with a long spiel about how he has known these kids all their lives and he wishes to help them out before his wicked board of directors makes him foreclose. He has a pocketful of documents and Goldberg lets him spread them all over the table.

The Doc and I are standing behind a set of curtains across a doorway and when Goldberg speaks up with his first, "No!" the Doc pokes me in the ribs and grins. When Crunchway gets up to fifty thousand I begin to relax.

Goldberg slaps the table. "We will sell our land, Jeff Crunchway," he says, "but we must have one hundred thousand dollars in cash. We do not trust your checks."

Ten minutes later we are doing a war dance around the room and I get a couple of sample hugs from Sharon that almost make me forget the heap of cabbage on the table.

She takes Goldberg by the arm and her voice is shaky. "I am so proud of you," she says. "You were splendid." She turns to us. "You are all splendid."

The Doc grins at her. "We are not in the clear yet. Although I do not think Crunchway will check up until morning. He will spend the evening figuring how he can wiggle out of this gentlemen's agreement he spoke about this afternoon." He thinks for a minute. "We shall remain here until dark. Then we will return the proprietor's vehicle to the hotel, pick up our luggage, and we will all board the *Golden Belle.*"

Goldberg points at the pile of cabbage on the table. "You gentlemen must take half of it," he says. "Without your assistance we would have nothing."

For the first time since I know him the Doc backs away from dough. "No," he says. "We will take our ten per cent." He glances at me and I nod at him. Ten grand will put us into action.

We spend the rest of the afternoon helping Goldberg and Sharon pack a few odds and ends and listening to the squawks that go up from the hired help when they learn Crunchway is their new boss. About seven o'clock I figure we better get moving. This flivver may throw a spavin and we may have to walk to town.

We have stowed the O'Toole luggage in the flivver and I am just helping Sharon into the seat when a loud rough voice sounds off behind me.

"A fine pack of thieves," this somebody says. "Don't move or you will regret it."

My hands are above my head and I am taller than I ever am in my life. I take a quick peek around. What I see ain't good.

JEFFERSON CRUNCHWAY is standing in the door of the shed. He is holding a cannon with a hole in the muzzle about the size of a subway tunnel.

Sharon lets out a squeal and I can hear the Doc draw in his breath. The Doc is no hand for gunplay. I don't have a quick answer to this either. A long time ago I find out I am not bullet-proof.

Crunchway steps forward. "Line up," he says, "and do not move your hands."

Goldberg is standing near the wall and as he steps forward he stumbles and his left foot slides sideways. I realize that Crunchway is standing square in front of the Horseman's Helper. I throw a cold sweat when I see Goldberg's foot hit a switch handle sticking out from the side of the machine.

The sudden noise of the motor on the Horseman's Helper startles Crunchway. As he turns his head two of the long pipes swing forward and a suction cup clamps on his right ear. Another pipe with a brush on the end fetches him a swipe across the face. It is a dandy brush and the bristles are stiff and hard. Two more of the pipes swing out and take a grip around Crunchway's middle.

Crunchway lets out a screech and drops the cannon. A few more pipes go into action and by the time I step in and jolt Crunchway on the chin with a right hook he is in no shape for a comeback. In fact I have to duck fast or the Horseman's Helper will give me the business also.

Goldberg kicks the switch again and picks up Crunchway's cannon. The Horseman's Helper slows down and the pipes swing back. The Doc is holding his haybelly and cackling like he will bust. It is a couple of minutes before I realize it is funny.

Crunchy is out cold. I turn to Goldberg. "Maybe you own a nice deep well?"

The Doc shakes his head. "He will cause us no more trouble," he says. "Crunchway realizes he is beaten or he would not have resorted to such desperate measures. This whole transaction has been strictly legitimate." He opens his suitcase. "Here is our last quart of bourbon, pony boy. Load Crunchway into his car and drive him into town. I think one more treatment will result in a complete cure. We will meet you aboard the boat."

WE ARE lined up along the rail of the *Golden Belle.* Sharon O'Toole is standing close beside me and I am pleased to notice the boat is rolling a little. She looks up at the Doc.

"However did Jeff Crunchway find out that you were working in our interest?"

"That was a stupid blunder on my part," the Doc tells her. "I asked the hotel proprietor the way to your plantation. Crunchway called at the hotel after he had secured title to your land and the proprietor told him where we had gone. Crunchway added it up and got the correct answer." He shakes his head. "Crunchway is not only smart, he is thoroughly unscrupulous. In fact I believe he intended to use that gun."

I stare at him. "You think he was going to bump us off?"

The Doc's big red face is sober. "Look at it from Crunchway's angle," he says. "He saw the luggage in the car. He knew the O'Tooles were leaving town with us. He could eliminate all four of us, hide the er—remains in a secluded spot and no one would ask any questions. He would have the money, the plantation, and vengeance." He looks at me. "I trust you gave Crunchway the full treatment?"

"Well," I tell him. "I am not sure I give him all that is coming to him. I dump most of that bottle of whiskey down his gullet and pour the rest of it on his clothes. Then I park his car at the back door of the county jail and tap his chin a couple of times to make sure he is fully relaxed."

Sharon shivers. "You are very strong, Mr. Allan," she says. "I am glad you did not injure him, though he deserves it."

I lean closer to her and harden the muscles in my arm, although I am speaking to Goldberg. "Tell me something," I say to him. "What does the Horseman's Handy Helper think it is doing when it goes to work on Crunchway?"

Goldberg shrugs. "I haven't the faintest idea," he says. He smiles. "I am just as pleased that we left the Horseman's Helper behind. I suspect that machine has more intelligence than its inventor."

The Doc chuckles. "I shall venerate the memory of the Horseman's Helper to the end of my days," he says. He glances at me and takes Goldberg by the arm. "Let us have a chat with the captain of this boat," he says. "I understand he is tired of life on the river and is saving up to buy a farm. We must warn him of the hazards of an agricultural existence."

A breeze has come up and the boat is rolling quite a lot. I have to put my arm around Sharon to steady her.

THE
DOCTOR
DEALS

"THIS IS A SWEET RACKET,
PONY BOY—A RELIGIOUS PITCH
AND A REAL ESTATE CAPER,
COOKED UP TOGETHER," THE
DOC TELLS ME. SO WE BECOME
GOAT WORSHIPERS, DISCIPLES
OF THE REVEREND JERRY TERRY
DERRYBERRY—A CRAZY WAY
TO GET A HAYBELLY ON YOUR
BANKROLL!

W **E ARE** at a slow mope when we hit the top of the hill. The way the Doc is puffing and wheezing I figure he will crack his windpipe. I step around a turn in the path and what I see nearly bowls me over.

A dame is standing on a flat rock about ten feet away. She is a medium-sized filly maybe twenty years old with big brown eyes and wavy hair. She is done up in slacks and blouse of heavy yellow silk and she shows more curves than a rollercoaster. I never expect to see a job like this in the middle of the Kentucky hills.

The Doc waddles around the bend and lets out a wheeze that blows the leaves along the ground. The dame spots us and hops off the rock like it is a hot griddle. A second later she is floundering in the brush.

When she takes this dive I notice she is wearing a pair of sandals that hook over the toe with a strap. She jumps to her feet but the sandals cross up again and she does another flop.

The Doc shoves me back and bends over her. "I hope you are not hurt badly, my dear," he says.

The dame rolls over and tries to smile. "I'm sorry to be so silly," she says, "but you startled me."

The Doc grins. "We are harmless citizens. We just attended the race meeting at Louisville and are heading east. We took the wrong road and, as it was getting late, we decided to follow this path hoping to find someone who could direct us."

The dame looks puzzled. "Then you don't know?"

The Doc opens his swayback coat so his white vest shows, takes off his black skimmer and parks on the rock. "I know that you are injured," he says. "I am Doctor Pierce of New York City. Let me have a look at that ankle."

OF COURSE the only degree the Doc ever gets in his life is when the cops put the arm on him and ask a lot of embarrassing questions but he is a pretty good rough-and-tumble sawbones, at that. He runs his big mitt over the dame's slim pasterns.

"As my young friend here, Mr. Allan, would say," he tells her, "you have bowed a tendon. In other words, you have a severe sprain but no bones are broken." He gets to his feet. "Of course we will assist you to your home."

The dame looks scared. "Oh, no," she says. "You can't. He wouldn't like it."

The Doc shrugs. "We can't leave you here. And you must not walk on that ankle."

The dame stares at his big, red face. "Perhaps it is for the best," she says. "I feel that I can trust you."

This does not surprise me. The Doc makes a good living for many years because people trust him. I grin at her. "How about me?"

She smiles. "You have a hard face for a young man, Mr. Allan," she says. "But I think you can be trusted—with a third party present." Her face sobers. "Where did you leave your car?"

Derryberry is standing there holding a gun on us. He has Doris
Bates by the waist and she is bound and gagged.

"In that cowtrack at the foot of the path," I tell her.

She speaks slowly. "You must do exactly as I say. Go back
down the path and drive your car between the twin boulders directly across the road. You will find another car but
there is plenty of room."

The Doc and the dame are still parked on the rock when
I get back. I take the Doc to one side. "Listen," I tell him.
"I don't like this setup. There is a wagon in the bushes
behind those boulders that set somebody back about
fifteen grand."

The Doc grins. "Take it easy, pony boy." He turns to the
dame. "Our charming companion is named Doris Bates,"
he tells me. "Doris and her widowed mother are living in

the valley just beyond under rather peculiar circumstances. I have asked her to delay her recital of these circumstances until your return."

Doris turns these big brown lamps on me. "Have you ever heard of the Reverend Jeremiah T. Derryberry?"

"Just a moment, my dear," the Doc says. "My question is perhaps irreverent, but what does the T. stand for?"

Doris shakes her head. "I don't know."

The Doc grins at me. "Five will get you fifty it is Terence."

"I don't believe it," I tell him. "Nobody would hang a name like that on a helpless brat."

The Doc chuckles. "Jerry Terry Derryberry," he says. "It's wonderful." He turns to the dame. "Go ahead. You have our earnest attention."

Doris smiles and then her eyes darken. "It is amusing to you," she says, "but it is stark tragedy to me. Derryberry, or the Sage, as his followers call him, is an evil creature. Sometimes I can hardly believe that the man is human."

"Well," I tell her, "I trust he is not human. He sounds like the corniest gag I ever hear. If this Jerry Terry Derryberry business is on the level I am ready to turn myself in."

Doris takes me by the arm. "You don't know how wonderful it is to talk to normal people again. I have spent three weeks in this awful place."

The Doc cuts in. "Let's have the story. It's getting dark."

DORIS STARES off into the distance. "Daddy left a lot of property, over a hundred thousand dollars. Mother has always been a weak person. Since Daddy died she has—well, she has become a little silly. You must understand. She is not crazy. Just foolish and weak.

"When the Reverend Derryberry came to town, she joined his group. At first I thought it was a harmless interest. When she told me she was turning all her property over to him I did not believe it."

The Doc narrows his eyes. "What's the pitch?"

Doris looks puzzled. "I don't understand."

"Look," I tell her, "what's the guy's caper? How does he build your old lady up for this score?"

She shakes her head. "It's such a fantastic thing," she says. She turns to the Doc. "You can't understand until you see for yourself. Help me down into the valley. Tonight they are dancing the Saraband to the Goat. When you see that, you will realize what I am going through."

The Doc grins. "The Saraband to the Goat—a phony religious pitch. I haven't seen one in years." He gets up. "Money, pony boy," he says to me. "I smell money."

"I smell trouble," I tell him. "But maybe there will be a couple of laughs around, at that." I get to my feet. "Do I carry the baggage?"

"Of course," the Doc says. "But remember this is business."

I lean over and lift Doris in my arms. She is not such a bad bundle. She slips an arm around my shoulder and I step along like a hackney.

WE ARE almost at the bottom when this fire lights up. Doris gives a little jump and I nearly drop her.

"We must hurry," she says. "The ceremony will begin in a few minutes."

The brush grows right up to the edge of this little clearing where the fire is blazing. We stop in the shadows about fifteen yards from the fire and what I see bugs my eyes out of my head.

A couple of dozen people are hopping around the fire in a long line like a chain gang. They are all wearing these yellow slack-and-blouse outfits and at first I have trouble telling the guys from the dames. The Doc lets his breath out in a low whistle.

"What an amazing spectacle," he says.

Doris is shivering and I set her down. "The man with the drum," she says. "That is Derryberry, the Sage."

I have been hearing this thumping for the past couple of minutes. Now I see this tall guy with a bushy black beard. He is standing on the other side of the fire tapping on a flat drum in his hand. I notice a black hole in the hill behind him. "What is that?" I ask her. "A cave?"

"Yes," she says. "There are three caves. The center one is where the Goat is kept. The Sage and the Guardians live there. The rest of us sleep in two caves a little way up the hill, the men in one and the women in the other."

"Well," I tell her, "if I do not see this nobody can make me believe it. What do those goofs around the fire think they are doing?"

"They are worshiping the Goat," she says. "In a moment the Guardians will light the torches in the cave and you will see the Goat."

Two lights spring up in the dark inside of the cave behind the fire. There is a thin curtain across the front but we can see through it. It is a life-size statue of a goat and it shines like gold. "What is it made of?" I ask the dame.

"We never see it except at night and through the curtain," she says, "but the Sage says it is solid gold."

The Doc chuckled. "Tell me, Doris," he says. "What does your mother get in exchange for turning her property over to this Sage, or Derryberry, or whatever his handle is?"

"He owns this valley," she tells him. "All of these people have turned over their property to the Sage and each of them gets title to a few acres of the land. They take an oath that they will share all the benefits of the valley equally."

The Doc chuckles. "A religious pitch and a real estate caper, cooked up together. This Derryberry is a hot operator." He thinks for a minute. "What benefits does he tell them they will share?"

"That is the fantastic part of it," she says. She leans forward. "The Sage is going to speak. You will hear him tell the story himself. He always tells it on nights when they dance the Saraband."

THE TALL guy with the beard has stopped patting the drum. He lifts his hands and turns toward the cave. He has one of these rumbling voices that you can hear for a block.

"Behold the Goat," he says.

The goofs stand still, lift their hands and bow at the statue. Derryberry turns on the voice again.

"Countless ages ago," he says, "this valley, the Cradle of the Goat, was the center of all knowledge and all power on the earth. The Goat, ancient bearded symbol of fertility and wisdom, has waited through the centuries for those destined to become worthy of this power and wisdom. With him have waited the golden images who lie under the soil of this valley." He lifts his hands.

"After many years of searching, I found this valley. It was given to me to raise the Goat from the earth that held him. I used my savings to buy this valley according to the laws of the land. Now you are sharing it with me. We have taken the sacred oath. 'From each according to his blessings; to each according to his needs.' We must toil and strive and study. We must become worthy to fulfill the ancient prophecy." He drops his hands and steps back to the entrance of the cave.

The goofs all get up and start filing past him so he can pat them on the head. The Doc gets up on his feet. "Take us over to the Sage," he tells The dame. "I think we will become members of this little flock."

I take him by the arm. "Look," I tell him. "Have a little sense. The ponies will be galloping in a couple of days. With the roll we are packing we can run those Pimlico bookies loop-legged."

The Doc chuckles. "I have a little plan in mind. If it is successful we will have enough dough to give those bookies the worst time they've had since the year of the Big Wind."

The Doc knows I am a sucker for his little plans. "O.K.," I tell him. "But let us not linger here. I wish to attack those bookies while their dough is crisp and fresh." I pick up Doris again and follow the Doc across the clearing.

A fat bag with pop eyes rushes up to us. "Oh, Doris," she says. "I have been so worried. Are you hurt?"

The Doc pulls off his black skimmer and bows at the fat bag. "Nothing serious, Mrs. Bates," he tells her. "Just a sprained ankle." He glances at the tall guy. "We did not wish to interrupt your little ceremony so we waited until you had completed it."

DERRYBERRY HAS a big, hook nose, and little, bright, black eyes. He reaches up and strokes his beard. "We are grateful to you for restoring our sister," he says. He shoots a dirty look at Doris. "But our sister knows she should not bring strangers into this valley. This is sacred ground."

The Doc moves over and looks Derryberry right in the eye. "This was an emergency," he says. He bows. "I am Doctor Pierce and this is my associate, Mr. Allan."

The tall guy bows back at him. "I am sorry we cannot offer you hospitality," he says.

The Doc shakes his head. "We hope for much more," he tells him. "Mr. Allan and I have long been students of the occult. We wish to join your group and share the ancient wisdom."

Derryberry frowns. "That is impossible," he says. "There are many rigid requirements to be met."

The Doc reaches into his clothes and hauls out his leather. "I understand that all property of members is placed in a common fund under your supervision," he says smoothly. "As it happens, Mr. Allan and I have our entire holdings in cash." He riffles a stack of bank-notes under Derryberry's beak. "We have between us about twenty-five thousand in cash. Will that fulfill your requirement?"

Derryberry glitters his eyes at the lettuce. He makes a slow reach and gathers it in. "It is sufficient." He holds out his mitt to me.

I start to let out a squawk but the Doc pokes me in the ribs. "Give, pony boy."

I figure the Doc knows what he is doing but I am not happy as I watch my roll disappear into Derryberry's clothes. I have a hunch it is the last time I will see it.

"What is the procedure now?" the Doc asks.

"You will spend the next three days in meditation," Derryberry says. "On the third day I will make a trip to the courthouse and have a deed drawn for your portion of the land. That evening I will return and we will hold the ceremony of initiation." He turns to one of the goofs. "Show our new brothers to the sleeping-quarters." He raises his hands again and goes into the cave.

The goofs crowd around us and I never see such a collection of odds and ends. They are all sizes but Doris is the only one who is not packing plenty of age. They don't say a word but they look at us like we just come out of a cage. Finally the goof Derryberry tells to put us away, comes over and takes the Doc by the mitt. "Come, brother," he squeaks.

This goof is a skinny party with no teeth and a fringe of white hair around his bald skull. On the way to the cave he tells us his real name is Socrates and that he lives a few hundred years ago in Greece.

"Well," I tell the Doc, "the way you toss our bankroll around I am beginning to think you figure you are Diamond Jim Brady or maybe Pittsburgh Phil."

The Doc chuckles. "I put the boomerang twist on that roll," he says. "It will come back."

THIS CAVE the he-goofs hive up in is about forty feet long by fifteen wide. The floor is sandy and the roof is dry. A bunch of little oil stoves are sitting along one wall and about a dozen folding cots are stacked in a corner. The place is lighted by a couple of old buggy lamps with big, brass bowls on the bottom.

Socrates hands us a couple of cots and half a dozen blankets.

"How about some groceries?" I ask him.

He shows me a pile of tin cans about ten feet high. "We have nice spring water, too," he tells me. "Right there in the bucket." He turns around and starts to scuttle out.

"Just a moment," the Doc says. "Tell us what you do to pass the time."

The goof pats his skinny mitts together. "We are always busy," he says. "We meditate and we listen to the Sage, but most of the time we dig."

The Doc keeps his face straight. "What do you dig for?"

Socrates peeks over his shoulder. "The golden images," he whispers. "The golden men. They are out there under the ground. We dig all day. Soon we will find them."

I grin at the Doc. "A couple of weeks digging all day and doing this roadwork around the fire every night and you will lose your haybelly."

The goof shakes his head. "We watch at night. The golden men walk in the valley in the dark." He giggles. "Last night I saw one of them. I saw where he went back into the ground, too. But I won't tell you." He cackles and runs out of the cave.

The Doc pulls his flask off his hip. "Bring over a couple of those tin cups and the bucket," he says. "We will take on a few doses of bourbon before we dine."

A couple of minutes later I feel better. "Look," I tell him, "I can't figure how these suckers stay in circulation long enough for Derryberry to put the arm on them. Why don't their relatives shake them down long ago?"

The Doc grins. "They are just a fancy brand of sucker, pony boy," he tells me. "You put these goofs in ordinary clothes and plant them back in their home towns and you could not tell them from the Rotary Club or the Chamber of Commerce." He takes a swallow out of his cup. "We must work fast. I think this pitch is ready for the payoff. That is why he grabbed our dough. He is operating on a strictly legal basis but he knows the Law will give him a bad time if they catch up with him before all those deals are completed. Once he has cashed in all the suckers' property and handed out deeds to the land he is in the clear." He chuckles. "Derryberry couldn't stand the sight of all that cash. He knew it was bait but he had to take it."

"I could stand the sight of my roll right now," I tell him. "I hope and trust I will see it again."

The Doc pats me on the shoulder. "You will see it," he says. "And it will have a haybelly."

THE NEXT couple of mornings the goofs shoulder picks and shovels and march off to the diggings right after breakfast. There is nothing for us to do but sit around and meditate. We do not see much of Derryberry as he spends most of his time in his cave. I get a good gander at this pair of Guardians and they are no bargain in my book. They are big and beefy and they look mean. Every time I try to peek into their cave one of them parts the curtain and gives me a dirty look.

I put in a little work on Doris. Her ankle is better but she cannot walk on it so she sits around on a rock in the sun most of the day. She turns out to be a nice kid but by no means smart. The second afternoon the Doc joins us.

"How far is it to a town?" he asks her.

"Crawford is about twenty miles from here," she says.

"Good," the Doc says. "Do you think your ankle will stand a trip over the hill tomorrow?"

She looks excited. "I'm sure I could make it. Are we leaving?"

The Doc glances at me. "Give her the keys to our car." He turns to the dame. "Listen carefully, Doris. I want you to leave before Derryberry departs tomorrow morning. Go to the best hotel in Crawford and stay in your room until the day after tomorrow. If we have not joined you by then, you must go to the sheriff and bring him here." He reaches in his clothes and hands her a couple of fifties. "This will take care of your expenses. We will bring your mother with us."

Doris is trembling a little, but she is game. "I will do exactly as you say." She looks up at him. "You will be careful? You won't get hurt?"

The Doc smiles. "I do not approve of violence, although I fear there will be a certain amount of it necessary. But you may be sure we will not be hurt—not unless I have lost my touch."

Doris heads off to the hill the minute the goofs leave for the diggings the next morning. I feel better. It is good to know we have someone on the outside looking after our interests.

Ten minutes later Derryberry comes out of his cave. He is wearing a business suit and he carries a bulging briefcase. He looks around for us but we are planted behind a bush on the hill above him. He hesitates for a few seconds but finally he trots off toward the hill.

The Doc looks at his watch. "We will give him half an hour."

The Doc never tells me the details of his little plans but I figure I am entitled to a couple of answers at this point. I glance over the equipment he has laid out on a rock—two pick handles, a coil of rope, a cup of water and an empty coffee can.

"Well," I tell him. "I suppose we bop the Guardians on the skull with the pick handles and truss them up with the rope. But how do we get close enough to them?"

The Doc picks up the coffee can. "Did you observe those old carriage lamps in our cave?" He opens the can and shows me a handful of gray powder. "Those are carbide lamps. When carbide is dampened with water it produces an inflammable gas. If this gas is confined it will explode. We are going to bomb the Guardians out of the cave."

THIS HOMEMADE pineapple works like a dream. We set fire to the curtains across the entrance to the cave and then toss in the coffee can. The Guardians come stumbling out and I bop them one-two. We shove them together and wind the rope around them until they look like a garlic sausage. Then we roll them into a corner of the cave.

This cave is maybe half the size of the one we have been parking in and it is fixed up very comfortable. There is a big brass bed in the back with the Goat parked on one side and a desk on the other. The Doc walks over to the desk.

"Unless I am mistaken we will find enough evidence here to put Derryberry at our mercy," he says. "He will be glad to make a deal with us when he returns." He starts pulling out the drawers and shuffling papers. I walk to the other corner and take a look at the Goat.

Of course I never believe this statue is solid gold but I am a little surprised when I find out it is nothing but tin covered with gilt paint. I rap on it with my knuckles and the Doc jumps about a foot. "What's that?" he says.

"This Goat," I tell him. "It is hollow."

"Of course," he says. "I should have thought of it." He shoves the desk drawers back in and walks around the brass bed. "There is nothing of importance in the desk. Derryberry is as smart as I figured him to be." He taps on the statue. "Have you got a can-opener in your pocket?"

"I've got a corkscrew," I tell him.

He grins. "There are six jugs of bourbon in that desk. We will have use for the corkscrew later." He runs his hands over the statue. "The head," he says. "It twists off like a cap on a toothpaste tube."

As I reach up and take hold of the horns I hear this step behind me. I turn my head and freeze.

Derryberry is standing there. He has Doris Bates by the waist and a bandana is tied around her wrists and another one around her mouth. He is holding a gun.

"So you have solved the mystery of the Goat, Doctor Pierce," he says softly. He pushes Doris over to the bed and she slumps down. He reaches into his pocket, throws me a big clasp knife and backs around against the wall. He jerks his head at the trussed-up Guardians on the floor.

"Cut my boys loose," he tells me. He smiles at the Doc. "I found your accomplice, Miss Bates, trying to start your car. Miss Bates is by no means an accomplished motorist."

I am watching the gun. I start slowly across the floor toward the Guardians. The Doc snaps at me.

"Hold it, pony boy. Don't cut those ropes."

Derryberry's bushy brows go up. "You are hardly in a position to give orders, Doctor Pierce."

The Doc smiles. "I am afraid you are being impulsive," he says. "Perhaps we should examine your position."

Derryberry narrows his little eyes until they are just slits. "My position is excellent," he says.

The Doc nods. "At the moment," he says. He points at the Guardians. "Your boys have been subjected to rough treatment. If they are freed they may commit an act of violence." He lowers his voice. "You are a clever man, Derryberry. Too clever to get into a position where you may become a fugitive from the Law." He smiles. "You and I are not men of violence. We are men of intellect—businessmen. You have a neat, little deal here and I have dealt myself in. I am sure we can reach some sort of an agreement."

Derryberry is thinking. He reaches a hand up to take a pull at his beard. It is the hand with the gun in it. I let the clasp knife go. It clips him square between the lamps and his head slaps against the wall.

I give him two in the middle before I nail him on the whiskers.

The Doc picks up the gun while I take the bandanas off Doris. I hop across and put the bandanas on Derryberry while he is quiet. I look over at the Guardians. They are both awake now so I slip them a couple of taps with the pick handle.

The Doc pats me on the shoulder. "That was a neat job, pony boy."

"That was a neat spiel," I tell him. I go over to the Goat and twist the head around. It takes both of us to shake it out on the floor. The Doc goes through the papers while I count the cabbage. It comes to a hundred and thirty-six grand, mostly big bills.

Derryberry is shaking his head now. He glares at us. "You will regret this," he says.

The Doc grins. "You were about to commit a grave error," he says. "We saved you from yourself." His red face sobers. "As I said a few minutes ago, we are businessmen. We are ready to make a deal with you." He parts the pile of cash in the middle and drops half of it back into the Goat. He shoves a couple of the papers in his pocket.

"This is the deal. We are splitting the take with you so far as the cash received to date is concerned. We are also taking with us the power of attorney you extracted from poor old Mrs. Bates. I note that you have been unable to cash any of her property as yet. Of course Doris and her mother will leave with us, but I do not think they will talk about this incident to anyone."

Derryberry stares at him. "But the rest of these people—all this other property—"

The Doc chuckles. "I have been trimming suckers all my life," he says. "The cry of the skinned sucker is music in my ears. You may complete your pitch with no further interference from us."

We have a little trouble getting Old Lady Bates over the hill. Derryberry roars like a bull when we tie him into the same bundle with his Guardians, and the old lady is plenty upset at the way we treat the Sage.

She quiets down after we get in the car and Doris leans over and speaks to the Doc. "What shall I do with her after we get home?"

The Doc shakes his head. "I might suggest a few quiet months in a sanatorium."

"Well," I tell Doris, "if you will take my advice you will get her a job on a section gang. After this pick-and-shovel workout Derryberry gives her, it will be a breeze."

THE DOCTOR'S TEST

THE DOC LIKES THE WINNAGOOK
COUNTY FAIR. HE LIKES IT EVEN
BETTER AFTER WE RELIEVE GOOD
EVENING ALBERT OF HIS PROG-
DIAG-NOSTICATOR AND SET UP
OUR OWN PITCH, HELPING THE
LOCAL HAWKSHAW TRACK DOWN
THE VULTURE, AND SELLING
ELIXIR AT A BUCK A THROW.

THE **SIGN** over the gate says: WINNAGOOK
COUNTY FAIR. The Doc can hardly hold still long
enough to bounce four bits for his ticket.

"Shake it up, pony boy," he tells me. "I do not want to
miss a minute."

It is only ten o'clock in the morning and from what I see
a guy with a glass eye can look this spread over in twenty
minutes, but I know this is the first County Fair the Doc
makes in many years.

A bunch of appleknockers with straw hats and button
shoes are moping in and out of a couple of big barns where
they display cows and pigs and such matters. The Doc skips
these attractions and hustles me toward a medium-sized
carnival at the rear of the lot. He sniffs the fog of dust that
hangs over the premises.

"The very air is invigorating," he says. "It takes me back
to my vanished youth."

"Well," I tell him, "things probably change since you
peddle rattlesnake oil around the carnival circuit during
your vanished youth. You would soon starve that haybelly
off your middle if you tried to make a living nowadays out
of that old caper."

The Doc shakes his head. "Five will get you fifty we find a modern version of the old snake-oil pitch. This generation is just as gullible as the suckers I used to trim." He points to a booth with a red banner over the top. "Take a look at that."

The banner reads:

THE PROG-DIAG-NOSTICATOR KNOWS ALL... CURES ALL FREE EXAMINATION WITHIN!

The Doc chuckles. "Prognosis, diagnosis," he says. "The whole spiel is on that sign."

A tall, skinny party is propped up against the door into the booth. As we approach he looks around. He has a long beak that turns up on the end like there is a clothespin on it. There is only one beak in the world like that.

"Hello, Albert," I say.

The tall guy squints at me. "Good evening, Mr. Allan," he says. "I did not expect to encounter you here."

I slip the Doc a wink. "This is Good Evening Albert," I tell him. "Albert is a night watchman around the racetracks for so many years that he always says 'good evening' no matter what time it is."

THE DOC opens his swayback coat so Good Evening Albert can get a gander at his white vest. He looks up at the banner. "Are you associated with this enterprise?"

"I am the sole owner," Albert tells him, "but I fear at present it is not an enterprise. The sheriff has just ordered me to cease and desist."

"Maybe you should slip a couple of crisp banknotes in this sheriff's pants pockets," I tell him.

Good Evening Albert stands with
his mouth open as I yank Heebner's
skimmer down over his eyes and
the Doc reaches for his cannons.

"The first two nights here I paid the sheriff ten dollars,"
Albert says. "Now he wants twenty. I do not average over
twenty dollars a night."

The Doc is interested. "On what grounds does he close
you up?"

"He claims I practice medicine without a license," Albert
says. "Of course that is not true. The only medicine I have
around the joint is a little aspirin for my personal use after
I interview these sheriffs."

The Doc scowls. "If there is anything I hate worse than
a copper, it is a crooked copper. There is plenty of competition around these days without the Law moving in." He
thinks for a minute. "Let's take a look at your pitch."

"Certainly," says Albert, opening the door.

I see some strange contraptions in my time but this Prog-what-you-call-it is out in front by ten lengths. It is a square white cabinet with a bunch of dials on top and four different colored lights, one at each corner. There is a chair with a pair of shiny steel cuffs hooked to the arms and a wire from each cuff to the cabinet.

"This chair gives me the creeps," I tell Albert. "It looks like the Hot Squat up at Sing Sing."

"It is harmless," Albert says. "Would you like to see it in action?"

The Doc parks in the chair. "Let's hear the spiel."

Good Evening Albert puts on a long white coat, clamps the shiny cuffs on the Doc's wrists and goes behind the cabinet.

"The functions of the human body are divided into four categories," he says, very brisk. "The anatomy, the physiology, the metabolism, and the circulation of the blood. With the Prog-diag-nosticator the trained mind can readily determine in which category your ailment is located." He throws a switch and the contraption hums like a swarm of bees.

"Well," I tell Albert, "I must say I am surprised to hear you put on a slick patter like this. Where do you round up all these five-dollar words?"

"Soapy Ginsberg taught me," Albert says. "Soapy has been operating the Prog-diag-nosticator for the past two years but now he has a combination can-opener and potato-peeler which he thinks has a great future. Soapy sold me this whole outfit, including the white coat, for three hundred dollars." Albert looks sad. "I have always wanted to be a gypsy and answer the call of the open road. All the years I was night-watching in the racing stables I saved my money and waited for just such an opportunity."

The Doc nods at a line of bottles on a shelf. "I suppose those jugs are the payoff?"

Albert nods back at him. He starts twisting the dials on top of the cabinet. "You are a very interesting case," he tells the Doc. "I would suggest that you cut down on starchy foods as you are considerably overweight." The purple bulb on the cabinet lights up. Albert takes down one of the bottles. "Elixir Number Three is indicated in your case. One dollar, please."

The Doc chuckles. "What are the components of this elixir?"

Good Evening Albert grins. "Plain water with a little flavoring. Soapy Ginsberg used to add a small amount of gin to make it more palatable but I cannot afford the expense."

"It is a nice little pitch," the Doc says. "Too bad you bump into this grafting sheriff. What are your plans now?"

"I am discouraged," Albert tells him. "There is a position open for night-watchman of this carnival. I intend to apply for it."

The Doc reaches for his wallet. "I will pay one hundred and fifty dollars for this outfit," he says. He lays three half-yard notes on the cabinet. "Take it or leave it."

Before I can open my mouth Albert pounces on the bills. He scribbles on a piece of paper. "Here is your bill of sale." He yanks off the white coat and heads for the door. "Thank you, sir," he says, "and good evening to you."

IT IS noon before we get all this gear stowed in the auto court cabin we are hived up in. Besides the chair, the cabinet and the electric motor that works the cabinet there are about thirty dozen bottles of Albert's remedies. The Doc parks on his bunk and mops his big red face. "Break out the bourbon, pony boy. We will have a quick dose before lunch."

I hand him a bottle. "How about a snort of Elixir Number Three?"

The Doc chuckles. "I am afraid the elixir is too weak for the purpose."

"I am afraid you are getting weak in the brain," I tell him. "We have six hundred dollars in the world and you throw away a yard and a half for this bunch of junk."

"I thought you had more imagination," the Doc says. "This outfit, with a few alterations, is exactly the equipment we need."

"O.K., I'll bite," I tell him. "Why do we need equipment?"

"We cannot possibly trim this sheriff with our bare hands," he says.

I go to my bunk and drag out my keester. The Doc grins. "The bourbon is in my suitcase," he says.

"I do not care for bourbon right now," I tell him. "I am lamming out of here before you get violent."

The Doc gets up and puts his hand on my shoulder. "You are not running out, pony boy? I have a tidy little plan in mind for this sheriff—with a fat payoff."

"Look," I tell him, "I go along with your little plans for years and I admit you cash out most of the time, but right now I have a date with a bunch of long-shots at Belmont Park. When I left home my old man gave me a piece of advice: 'Never carry a bundle by the string,' he told me, 'and never pick a cop's pocket.' My old man is a smart guy."

"I'm sure he is," the Doc says. He reaches in his keester for the bourbon. "Have a couple of snorts with me before you go and I will outline my little plan."

"O.K.," I tell him. "I am in no hurry. Maybe I can slip you a few suggestions."

The next morning I wake up with the sun in my eyes. The Doc has broken out his best striped pants and a fresh white vest. He is also dusting off his black skimmer and his swayback coat. He grins at me.

"Rise and shine, pony boy," he says. "We have a busy day before us."

I give him a sour look. "If my old man knew that I let you talk me into this goofy caper he would knock my brains out with a baseball bat."

The Doc chuckles. "You can send your daddy a diamond stickpin when this pitch pays off." He glances across the room. "What do you think of the result of our labors?"

I have to grin. Even Soapy Ginsberg will not recognize his contraption now. The night before we change the cabinet around so the dials are on the side. We also saw off the legs and give it a coat of black enamel. "I hope you think up a simple name for this gadget," I tell him.

"We will call it the Salivator." The Doc goes over and taps the paint. "It will be dry in a couple of days. I expect to take at least that long to line up this pitch."

THIS WINNAGOOK is a pretty town with trees along the streets and a brand-new courthouse with a big cupola on top. I slow down and steer the crate over to the curb.

The Doc looks up at the building. "Apparently pickings are good for the courthouse boys."

"Did you notice those bars on the basement windows?" I ask him. I am always nervous within reaching distance of a jail.

The Doc slaps me on the back and gets out of the car. "Take it easy, pony boy. Remember you are a distinguished scientist."

This hayshaker hawkshaw is not in his office but a blond bag of rags in a little room outside says we can wait inside. The office is big and clean and the chairs are soft. I am beginning to relax when this big moose comes in.

"Hello, folks," he booms at us. "I am Josh Heebner, Sheriff of Winnagook County." He puts out a mitt the size of a saddlebag.

I have been here and there but I never see a sight like this Sheriff Josh Heebner. He is two inches taller than the Doc and is packing twenty pounds more weight although he is maybe ten years younger.

He is wearing a flat-brimmed skimmer with a peaked crown, a bright plaid shirt, a leather vest, a pair of khaki britches and shiny leather puttees. He also has two big cannons buckled on his hips and a pair of black sideburns halfway down his fat cheeks. He looks like a cross between Wild Bill Hickok and an overstuffed Boy Scout.

The Doc bows. "I am Dr. Pierce of Washington, D.C., and this is my associate, Dr. Allan."

Heebner sits down behind the desk. "What can I do for you gents?" He has shiny teeth and he smiles but his little black eyes do not smile. They watch the Doc like a hawk.

The Doc hitches his chair up close to the desk. "We have a most confidential matter to discuss with you." He takes a peek over his shoulder. "I trust you do not have a dictaphone concealed in here?"

Heebner laughs until the windows rattle. "I got no use for contraptions like that. We don't have bad criminals here."

The Doc looks sad. "I am sorry to disillusion you," he says, "but your fair community is harboring one of the worst fiends in criminal history." He lowers his voice. "Have you ever heard of the Vulture?"

Heebner shakes his head. "No, I ain't."

The Doc nods. "Very few people have. His existence is almost a secret." He thinks for a minute. "You have a reputation as an honest and capable officer of the law. I think we can be frank with you, and when the reward money is collected I am sure you will be fair with us."

Heebner sits up. "There's a reward for this Vulture?"

"The Government is offering ten thousand for his capture," the Doc tells him. "Dead or alive."

"Ten thousand dollars?" Heebner's eyes stick out like marbles.

"That's only part of it," the Doc tells him. "The insurance companies have offered another ten and three private parties have put up five apiece making a total of thirty-five thousand dollars."

Heebner grabs at the cannons on his hips. "You say this Vulture is around here? I'll have him in jail so fast—"

The Doc interrupts. "It will not be so easy," he says. "The Vulture has a low bestial cunning. He has outwitted the cleverest police officers in the country. In fact, until a few weeks ago we did not have the slightest clue to his identity." The Doc glances at me. "Now, thanks to the brilliant work of my young colleague here, we have such a clue."

Heebner is thinking. "You fellers Federal agents?"

"In a way, yes," the Doc tells him. "We are research scientists. We work closely with the Secret Service although we are not actually a part of it. You might say we are the Secret Secret Service. We carry no badges or credentials and operate independently. We report only to the Chief himself and draw our salaries and expense money from his emergency fund."

Heebner chews on this. "Sounds kind of funny," he says. He reaches for the phone. "Maybe I better call Washington and check up on you fellers."

I GET ready for a quick lam out the door but the Doc smiles. "Very well," he says, "but if you call Washington you'll have a dozen Federal men here in the morning. They'll grab the Vulture and you'll be out in the cold."

Heebner puts down the phone. "What you mean?"

"I'll explain briefly," the Doc says. "We members of the Service are not allowed to accept rewards. We brought this to you because you are in a position to make the arrest and also collect the reward. We can always use a little extra money. We want fifteen thousand of the thirty-five. You keep the rest."

Heebner nods. "Sounds fair enough."

The Doc slips him another helping. "Of course we must trust to your honesty. There is no way we can force you to pay us our share and of course you will get full credit in the papers for the capture of the Vulture."

The way Heebner looks when he hears this I will not trust him around the corner. He licks his lips. "This Vulture. What's he done and how do we grab him?"

The Doc looks solemn. "The Vulture is a beast in human form. He attacks his prey with a butcher's cleaver. When life has left the hacked body he kneels on his victim's chest and gouges out his eyes. He drools and slobbers all the time he is engaged in his fiendish task. That is the clue that will lead us to him."

Heebner gives a shudder and I am not too comfortable, even though I know the Doc just dreams this Vulture up out of thin air. "Where do these killings take place?" Heebner asks.

"In various large cities," the Doc tells him. "The police in each city thought it was a local criminal. It was not until the Vulture made his fatal mistake and we took over the case that it was discovered the crimes were the work of one man."

Heebner is panting. "What mistake?"

"He stole a sealed, stamped envelope out of a victim's pocket," the Doc says. "That is a Federal offense."

Heebner nods. "What's this clue you got?"

"Saliva," the Doc says. "As I told you, the Vulture drools and slobbers over his victims while he is gouging their eyes out. We simply collected samples of his saliva."

"What good's that?" Heebner says. "You can't tell nothing from spit."

"That used to be true," the Doc says. He shoots a look at me. "My brilliant young friend here, Dr. Allan, is an expert on saliva. He developed the saliva test for race-horses. Many examples of chicanery around the tracks have been discovered as a result of his work."

Heebner nods and I try to look brilliant. "I heard tell about that stuff," he says.

The Doc goes on: "After months of experiment Allan has developed an apparatus that breaks down the components of individual human saliva. The test is even more accurate than the fingerprint method of identification." The Doc peeks around the room again. "Of course I am betraying a Government secret in telling you this. The criminal world has not yet heard of the Salivator."

Heebner is hooked. "How do you know this Vulture is in Winnagook County?"

The Doc shakes his head. "I am afraid that is a little professional secret we cannot divulge." He points his finger at Heebner and speaks very low. "The Vulture is not only in Winnagook County, he is right in this building. He may even be a member of your staff."

Heebner gives a shiver. "Shucks," he says. "I've knowed everybody around here since they was pups."

"That is why it has taken us so long to track the Vulture down," the Doc says. "He poses as a normal, respectable citizen."

Heebner shivers again. He reaches in his desk and hauls out a square bottle. "I need a drink. Will you gents join me?"

I move over to the desk and we click the glasses. "To the capture of the Vulture," the Doc says. "And to the thirty-five thousand-dollar reward."

HEEBNER GULPS the whiskey. "How you figure on getting these samples? Everybody don't spit where you can get at it."

"We have a plan," the Doc says. "But we must have the cooperation of the county authorities."

Heebner pours himself another dose. "Judge Keppler is the big gun around here. Him and me runs this courthouse."

"Splendid," the Doc says. "Just introduce us to the judge as friends of yours from the State Department of Health."

Heebner scowls. "You ain't going to cut the judge in on this reward?"

"Of course not," the Doc says. "There is hardly enough to go around as it is."

Heebner's little eyes glitter. "That's what I was thinking," he says slowly and he grins.

This Judge Keppler is an old fat slob with about eight chins sliding down his vest. The Doc tells him that there is an epidemic of human hoof-and-mouth disease and the State has sent us to examine the courthouse employees.

"I shall be honored to assist you in this vital work," the judge says.

"Fine," the Doc tells him. "We have prepared a gargle which indicates the presence of the disease. We want every person in the courthouse to use this gargle and deposit a mouthful in a paper cup. We will examine these specimens in the State Laboratory. For those who wish to take preventive measures against the disease we will furnish a mouthwash, made up by the State at cost. One dollar a bottle."

The Judge bows. "I will pass the word around to all the offices," he says. "I am sure you will find everyone glad to help."

In the hall outside the sheriff pokes the Doc in the ribs. "You are a man after my own heart," he says. "Never miss a chance to make an extra dollar." He cackles. "Be sure and get a dollar for the mouthwash from Judge Keppler. I like to put one over on that old scoundrel."

I spend the next two days with the white coat on, gargling the courthouse help. We have quite a flock of these paper cups as there are a couple of hundred employees. The Doc trots around after me putting on a quick spiel and collecting dollars for these bottles of mouthwash which of course are the stock he buys from Good Evening Albert along with the contraption.

The third day I have everybody covered and the Doc has peddled the last bottle of elixir. He gets rid of the extra stock by telling the employees they should take a bottle home for the protection of their families. We move the cabinet from the auto camp into a room in the best hotel in town.

Right after lunch we bring Heebner up to the room. His eyes pop out when he sees the contraption and he is very quiet while I fiddle around with the paper cups and make noises with the electric motor. We let him sweat for a couple of hours and then I come from behind the cabinet with a paper cup in my mitt. We have these cups numbered.

"Here it is," I yell. "This is the Vulture."

THE DOC'S face is very solemn and I think Heebner is going to bust a surcingle. The Doc takes a peek at the number on the cup, puts on his cheaters with the black ribbon and opens his notebook. He stares at the pages for a long time and then turns to Heebner.

"You have a sad duty to perform, my friend," he says.

Heebner gets out a bandana and wipes his fat face. "Who is it?" he croaks.

The Doc shuts his notebook and shakes his head. "Under the circumstances I cannot divulge the identity of this foul creature at this time. The consequences might react on all of us." He thinks for a minute and shakes his head again. "No," he says. "The Chief would not like it." He turns to Heebner. "I think it best that Allan and myself leave town before you make this arrest."

Heebner has his mouth open but he can't say a word.

The Doc pats him on the shoulder. "We must be very careful. I have my responsibility to the Chief in Washington." He starts walking up and down the room. He snaps his fingers. "I have it." He turns to Heebner. "Does the local bank have a time lock on the safe deposit vault?"

Heebner bobs his head up and down.

"Good," the Doc says. "You must do exactly as I say. We will deposit this cup with the sample of saliva from the Vulture's mouth in a safe deposit vault which cannot be opened until tomorrow morning. I will also place a sealed envelope in the box with the name of the Vulture and the address of our Chief in Washington. When you make the arrest tomorrow morning you must immediately wire the Chief. He has the reward money and is authorized to pay it. Allan and I will leave here tonight and report to the Chief. He will furnish whatever assistance is necessary to convict the Vulture and he will pay you the reward."

Heebner thinks it over. "You think I'll have any trouble arresting this Vulture?"

"Not a bit," the Doc tells him. "He does not suspect anything and he is perfectly harmless without his cleaver."

Heebner nods his head. "Sounds all right to me. I'll take plenty of help along when I nab him." His little eyes glitter.

The Doc gives Heebner a look. "Of course we trust you," he says. "But I think we should have a small token payment just as evidence of good faith, say five thousand. You can mail us the other ten out of the reward."

"I ain't got that much cash handy."

The Doc looks sad. "Perhaps we had better call in the Federal agents after all. Maybe we could work something out with them."

Heebner grabs the Doc's arm. "Don't do nothing hasty," he says. "We worked together good so far." He thinks for a minute. "Maybe I can borrow it from Judge Keppler. He's always well heeled."

"We will go to the bank together first," the Doc says. "Then you can meet us here at five o'clock with the money."

HEEBNER HAS the five grand in fresh bills. The Doc stuffs it into his leather. "We will expect to hear from you in the near future," he says. "You may be sure we will tell the Chief of your splendid work. Perhaps he can find a place for you on his staff."

Heebner grins. "I'm doing all right," he says. "I got the voters sewed up and I know every turn in the road around this county." He shakes hands with us and starts out. Just as he has his hand on the knob there is a loud rap. Heebner opens the door and Good Evening Albert walks into the room.

"What have you done to the Prog-diag-nosticator, Mr. Allan?" Albert says, very loud. "You have ruined it with that black paint." He turns to the Doc. "I found out you were still here and I came up to buy it back. I do not want that night-watching job and I have a fine idea for changing it around so these lousy sheriffs will not bother me."

I am watching Heebner and I see this ugly look come on his face. "You dirty crooks," he says. He reaches for the guns on his hips.

As his hands move I pull his Boy Scout skimmer down over his ears and eyes. It is a tight fit and he squawks and grabs at the hat. The Doc has the pair of cannons. I pull Heebner's leather vest down to his elbows and we spin him into the closet and slam the door.

Good Evening Albert is standing with his mouth open. The Doc hands him the guns and I grab our keesters and head for the door. "Beat it, quick, Albert," the Doc says. "You can open a shooting gallery."

I am hand-riding the crate down the highway expecting to hear a siren behind us any minute. The Doc chuckles. "You seem nervous, pony boy."

"Sure," I tell him. "I am waiting for the Heebner drag-net to close in."

"There will be no drag-net," the Doc says. "Heebner is too smart to squawk. The voters would laugh him right out of that courthouse."

I shiver. "I will never forget his face when Albert walks into that room."

The Doc chuckles again. "I wish we could see Sheriff Josh Heebner's face when he opens that deposit box tomorrow morning and finds out the Vulture is nobody but good old Judge Keppler."

THE DOCTOR'S SWITCH

PROFESSOR SPEEVLE IS NOT A
SAWBONES. HE CALLS HIMSELF
A HEALTHICIAN AND CLAIMS HIS
TREATMENTS WILL PATCH UP
ANYBODY WHO HAS NOT HAD
HIS THROAT CUT. THE DOC AND I
ARE UP AT HIS SANATORIUM—BUT
NOT FOR OUR HEALTH. THERE'S
A SMALL MATTER OF FIVE GRAND
TO TAKE CARE OF AND ALSO
WE GOTTA RESCUE MAYBELLE,
OLD SPEEVLE'S CURVACEOUS
DAUGHTER, FROM A FATE WHICH,
SO THEY TELL ME, IS FAR WORSE
THAN DEATH.

THE REASON I can see over the top of the bushes along the shore is because I am in the hind end of this canoe. The Doc and his haybelly are in front so I am sitting about three feet up in the air.

We are not showing much speed. The Doc is supposed to be an invalid and he is too fat to paddle anyhow. And every time I try to reach the water with my paddle the Doc lets out a yell and claims I am tipping the boat over. I can't figure why he is scared as he is bound to float like a cork.

I take a quick gander over the top of the bushes, lean forward and speak in a low voice. "Here is a peculiar sight. This Howland Rutherford Chenery is stepping along through the woods as lively as a two-year-old."

The Doc pushes his wide black skimmer off his forehead and turns slowly so as not to wiggle the canoe. His big red face is puzzled. "That is indeed peculiar," he says. "Only an hour ago I observed Mr. Chenery coming out of the dining room. He was walking with great difficulty and leaning heavily on his cane."

"Well, he is not leaning on anything now," I tell him. "In fact he is spinning this cane like a drum major and whacking leaves off the bushes."

Cornelius Potts steps out of the closet, a long-barreled Roscoe in his hand. "I heard that little attempt at blackmail," he says, grim-faced.

The Doc looks thoughtful. "Can it be possible that Mr. Chenery is guilty of deliberate deception as to his physical condition?"

"I have heard of characters who stoop to such low trickery," I tell him. "In fact I can poke such a party with my paddle from here."

The Doc frowns. "This may be serious, pony boy. Mr. Chenery strikes me as an astute and capable young man. If he is going to furnish competition it may be well to alter the little plan I have in mind. In fact, I think we had better step up the schedule and make this pitch immediately."

OF COURSE I do not know exactly what the Doc has in mind as he never lets me in on the details of his little plans until they are ready to pay off, but I know that we are not up here in the hills at Speevle's Sanatorium for our health. Even though the Doc lets on to Professor Ellsworth Speevle that his health is very bad.

"This is good news," I tell the Doc. "In fact if we do not get into action soon I will get as rusty in the joints as you and the other inmates of this mausoleum." Of course I only say this to give him the needle. The Doc is fifty-odd and packs plenty of weight for his age but he is as healthy as a horse. In fact, he has a lot more zip and go than many horses I have seen running around racetracks.

The Doc lets it go by. "Yes," he says, "we will move in on Professor Speevle today. I have had my suspicions of Mr. Chenery and what you have just seen confirms them. We cannot afford to wait until he makes his pitch, whatever it is. The good professor might slice very thin if too many people work on him at once."

"How soon do we come to the payoff?" I ask him.

The Doc grins. "If my little plan works out, we will be on the noon train from Hoedown Junction tomorrow, with a bundle of Professor Speevle's banknotes in our pockets."

This is very good news. We are only holding about a grand between us and it costs fifteen iron men per day to stay in this dump. And outside of these high altitude canoe trips with the Doc there is no excitement going. Speevle's Sanatorium is a rambly old shack on the shore of this lake and there is not a thing in the vicinity except a lot of trees that come down and peek in the window at night.

The customers are old pelters, mostly dames, that should have had their shoes pulled years ago. They spend their time churning around in the mud baths, lapping up mineral water and sitting on the porch telling each other how Professor Speevle says they have the biggest spavins he ever sees in his life.

Of course the Doc has to let on that he is broke down, too, or he will not have any reason for showing up at this place. He tells Professor Speevle that he is a well-known explorer and spends many years poking around in jungles and deserts. The Doc claims that all this poking around brings on a condition that calls for attention from Professor Speevle and his mineral water and mud baths. This Professor Speevle is not a sawbones or even a regular professor. He calls himself a healthician and claims his treatments will patch up practically anybody who has not had his throat cut.

The Doc puts me away as a party who is handy at writing books and he says he brings me along to help him record the things that happen to him in these jungles and deserts he has explored.

I have a hard time keeping my face straight when I hear the Doc shoot this spiel to Professor Speevle. The only exploring the Doc ever does in his life is in other people's wallets. And the only writing I ever tackle is letters to my old man biting him for a few dollars.

I even give that up after a couple of tries as my old man writes letters back that will make a loan shark bust out crying. In fact, I run a very poor second to my old man when it comes to putting on the bite and I always end up by sending him a sawbuck or two to help him out of his misery.

CORNELIUS POTTS is standing on the platform when we finally make it to the boathouse. Cornelius is a party about my age with a round haircut, big muscles, and freckles all over his face. He takes care of the canoes and does most of the heavy lifting around the sanatorium. He also spends a lot of time looking googly at Maybelle Speevle, the old professor's only child.

Maybelle is also standing on the platform and she grabs my end of the canoe while Cornelius is helping the Doc onto the platform. I am glad Maybelle is there because when the Doc and his haybelly leave the front, my end of the canoe comes down in the water with a whap. Also Maybelle Speevle is not a bad type of filly.

She is maybe twenty-two years old, legged up good with plenty of daylight under her, and she is rounded off in the right places. In fact, the first few days we are at the sanatorium I put in considerable work on Maybelle. I am going strong and getting plenty of dirty looks from Cornelius Potts when this Howland Rutherford Chenery arrives on the scene.

Chenery is a good-looking party a few years older than me, maybe thirty. He has slick black hair, long eyelashes and a sharp line of chatter. I never have any truck with him, partly because he takes dead aim at Maybelle right away, and partly because I do not like characters who put grease on their hair.

It turns out that Maybelle is very much in favor of this Chenery and in no time at all I am standing flat-footed at the post alongside Cornelius Potts. Maybelle trots around after Chenery like he has a lump of sugar in his pocket. Especially when the word gets around that Chenery has a large number of dollars in the bank and owns various properties such as oil wells.

Maybelle gives me a hand out of the boat and a smile. "How is Dr. Pierce's book coming along, Mr. Allan?"

"Just dandy," I tell her. "We have just got to the part where Dr. Pierce is lost in the desert and nearly dies of thirst because he loses his corkscrew. He is finally rescued by a tribe of friendly bartenders."

Maybelle laughs and even Cornelius Potts gives a snicker. I am a little surprised at this as it is the first time I notice Cornelius catching on to anything but the end of something heavy he is lifting.

The Doc doesn't like it. He gives me a scowl. "I must take my mud bath and drink my quota of mineral water," he says. "Meet me in my room in one hour." He heads for the main building with Maybelle trotting along beside him. I figure she is looking for Howland Rutherford Chenery and his long eyelashes and I wonder what she will think if she knows he is strictly a phony.

I help Cornelius Potts pull the canoe out of the water and put it up on a rack in the boathouse. Cornelius stands and looks at me for a minute and I can see he has something on his mind.

"Could I ask you a question, Mr. Allan?" he says.

"Sure," I tell him. "Go right ahead."

He shuffles his feet. "I hear you are a well-known author," he says. "I try to do a little writing in my spare time and I thought maybe you could give me a couple of tips."

Well, I can probably give him a better tip on the third race at Belmont but I figure this is no time to mention it. "What do you wish to know?"

"About the narrative hook," he says. "Just how do you handle it?"

"I never have any truck with it at all," I tell him. "Although a few years back when I am a fair lightweight they tell me I have a snappy left hook."

Cornelius gives a little grin. "Thank you, Mr. Allan. That is all I wanted to know."

Well, I can't make any sense out of this remark but I have other things to think about. "That's O.K.," I tell Cornelius.

"Any time you wish further information do not hesitate to call on me."

"You may be sure I will," he says. He still has this grin on his face.

WHEN I walk into the Doc's room an hour later he is all spiffed up in a fresh white vest and his best pair of striped pants. He is getting into his swayback coat and is full of ginger.

"This will be one of the quickest pitches we ever pull off, pony boy," he tells me. "I have it on good authority that Professor Speevle keeps a large sum of ready cash in the bank in Hoedown Junction. I have sent word to the good professor that we wish to speak to him in his office on a matter of importance. He is waiting for us now."

Of course I am anxious to get into action but I begin to feel nervous, like I always do when a caper is coming up.

"This is a bad setup for a quick getaway if anything goes wrong," I tell him. "There is only one train a day from Hoedown Junction and that is twenty miles from here. I would hate to hoof those twenty miles."

The Doc chuckles. "Professor Speevle's chauffeur, Herman, will drive us to Hoedown Junction in style," he says. "This pitch is practically airtight."

I feel better, although I have seen airtight capers before that turned out to be full of leaks. "What part do I play in this performance?"

"Just sit still and nod once in a while," the Doc says. "I do not anticipate a situation that will call for your particular talents."

Professor Speevle is a rosy-cheeked old pappy with a short white beard and shiny blue eyes behind thick cheaters. He gives us a big greeting and parks us in a couple of chairs across a big table. "The healthician treatment is working wonders for you," he tells the Doc. "You are much better."

"I feel fine," the Doc says. "But it is not due to your treatment." He reaches in his pocket and lays a card on the table. "I have some bad news for you, Professor. This will explain."

Speevle's eyes bug out as he reads the card. He stares at the Doc and his cheeks are not so rosy. "Then you are not an explorer, Dr. Pierce," he says finally. "You are an M.D. and chief investigator for the Amalgamated Medical Society."

"That is correct," the Doc says. He nods at me. "And Mr. Allan is not an author—he is a laboratory technician."

This is all news to me but I sit up straight and try to look like a laboratory whatsis.

The Doc goes on, his voice solemn: "As chief investigator for the society, my function is the investigation of establishments such as your sanatorium. I regret to inform you that you are not only violating the principles of good practice but that some of your methods place you in definite jeopardy in the eyes of the law."

Speevle's cheeks are dead white now. "The law?"

The Doc nods. "Mr. Allan's analysis of your mineral water and mud baths shows that they are definitely harmful. To put it bluntly, you are liable to prosecution under the criminal and civil statutes of this state on at least nine counts."

Speevle plucks at his beard. "Nine counts!" His hands are shaking and I figure it is all over except passing the hat for the money.

The Doc nods again. "Each count carries a jail sentence and a substantial fine." He lowers his voice. "You have a good business here, Professor Speevle, and I would hate to see you lose it. Mr. Allan and I are reasonable men. It is just barely possible that we might arrange to have your establishment put on the approved list." He pauses for a moment and lets it sink in. "Of course, we would expect a fairly substantial fee for our services."

Speevle looks the Doc straight in the face. "How much?"

I am breathing heavy and sweating a little but the Doc does not bat an eye. "Five thousand dollars, cash on the line by eleven o'clock tomorrow morning. We will depart on the noon train."

Speevle speaks in a loud voice. "Five thousand dollars! Why, this is an outrage," he says.

The Doc shrugs. "If you think our terms exorbitant we will have to let the law take its course. The Society will start legal action immediately."

Speevle turns to a closet behind him and yanks the door open. "Did you hear everything?" he asks.

CORNELIUS POTTS steps out of the closet. He is carrying a long-barreled roscoe in his hand and his freckled face is grim. "I heard this little attempt at blackmail," he says. He points the gun at me. "Narrative hook," he says. He gives a little snort. "I have suspected you were an imposter for some time," he tells me. "Our little chat in the boathouse convinced me. I told Professor Speevle that you two were up to something crooked. So we set a little trap and you fell into it."

The Doc looks puzzled. "I fail to see where you fit into this discussion, Mr. Potts," he says. "And I must say I fail to comprehend your remarks. What is all this about a narrative hook?"

Cornelius smiles. "You are clever, Dr. Pierce," he says. "I must admit that you took me in. But when you tried to pass this Broadway bumpkin off as an author it was a little too much to swallow." He turns to me. "I happen to be a fairly successful writer myself, Mr. Allan. I spend my summers here because I like the fresh air and exercise. For your information, a narrative hook is a device by which a writer pulls a reader into his story. When you displayed your ignorance of the term I knew you were an imposter."

The Doc puts on a big smile. "The fortunes of war," he says. "It seems we have over-matched ourselves again." He gets to his feet. "We will bid you good day, and good-by."

Cornelius shakes his head. "You have just made a bare-faced attempt at extortion. I think we will hand you over to the sheriff."

I figure it is time to make a move. I measure the distance to Cornelius' big chin and get set. He has twenty pounds on me but I figure it is worth a try. I glance at the Doc and I am very much surprised when he gives me the office not to start anything. He keeps this big smile on his face and shakes his head at Cornelius.

"You are an intelligent young man, Mr. Potts," he says. "But I fear you have not examined this situation thoroughly. Both Mr. Allan and I are respectable citizens. We have never been arrested. If you attempt to push this charge of extortion we will simply deny everything. Furthermore we will sue for false arrest and defamation of character. It will be our word against yours."

It is a good quick spiel and I can see it sinking in on the professor and Cornelius. They look at each other and Speevle shakes his head.

"It is a great pity," he says. "But I suppose we will have to let them go. A scandal of this sort would be bad for business."

Cornelius is thinking hard. "Perhaps you are right, Professor," he says. "But I still think we should have them arrested. In the first place I do not believe they are connected with the Medical Society at all. In fact, I doubt if Dr. Pierce is even a physician."

The Doc chuckles. "My medical background will stand the closest scrutiny," he says. "In fact, now that I think it over, I would welcome arrest. We can certainly collect at least five thousand dollars in damages."

I BREAK out in a cold sweat when the Doc comes up with this line. The only medical background he ever encounters in his life is when he peddles snake oil around the carnival pitches some years back.

Cornelius frowns. "I believe you are bluffing. In fact, I am sure of it." He thinks for a moment, suddenly he smiles. "Set a thief to catch a thief," he says in a soft voice, almost to himself. He puts the gun back in his belt and sits down at the table. "With the professor's permission, I'm going to make you two rascals a sporting proposition." He glances at Speevle. "I think perhaps Dr. Pierce can furnish a solution to the Chenery problem."

Speevle stares. "I don't understand. What can he do?"

"Show him up." Cornelius turns to the Doc. "It may interest you to know that you are not the only bogus patient at the sanatorium."

The Doc is interested. "We know that Mr. Chenery can walk without his cane. Mr. Allan observed him stepping briskly through the woods this afternoon." He looks at the professor. "Just what sort of problem does Mr. Chenery present?"

Speevle's face is very sad. "He has captured my daughter's affections, for one thing," he says. "And Cornelius and I are convinced that he is a shady character. I don't know what his original purpose in coming here was, but he is going to steal my daughter. Maybelle and I had a very stormy scene last night. She informed me that she is determined to go away with Chenery. She says they are to be married but that Chenery does not want to have the ceremony performed here. I tried to point out that an honest man would have no objection to marrying her here but she wouldn't listen. She is wholly under his influence." He shakes his whiskers. "Maybelle is of age and I cannot prevent her from taking this terrible step."

Well, I am not surprised when I hear this as Maybelle strikes me as being on the dumb side, even for a dame. I look at Cornelius. "Why don't you just put the slug on Chenery and pop him in the lake some evening?" I say. "Then you can take dead aim at Maybelle without any competition."

Cornelius gets red and the Doc slips me a quick look. "You are out of order, pony boy," he says. "This is a serious situation." He thinks for a minute. "Do you gentlemen have any idea of what Chenery had in mind when he showed up here?"

Cornelius shakes his head. "Not the slightest, except that I am sure it was something clever. The professor thinks that he has abandoned his original intention and is mostly interested in Maybelle. I do not agree with him."

"Neither do I," the Doc says. "Chenery strikes me as a smart operator. He will make his pitch and scoop up the girl with the same motion." He thinks for a minute. "Frankly, I am curious about Chenery. I would like to know what he is up to." He glances at the professor. "Mr. Allan and I will be pleased to undertake the task of exposing this rascal."

Cornelius smiles. "Good. What steps do you propose?"

The Doc gets to his feet. "We will wait until Chenery makes his move. I think he will not delay much longer. The instant he comes to you with any kind of proposition, notify us immediately. We will handle it from there." He bows at Speevle and Cornelius and we walk out.

CHENERY MAKES his move the next day. Professor Speevle and Cornelius come to the Doc's room after dinner. We are sitting around a bottle of bourbon and the Doc brings out a couple more glasses. Speevle is so excited he nearly dumps his drink on the carpet.

"Chenery claims to be cured," he tells us. "He came into my office a few minutes ago without his cane and told me that my treatment had performed a miracle. He also said that he hoped I was not too upset at the idea of his marriage with Maybelle.

"He was very plausible and claimed that due to business, he must make a long trip immediately and that they could be married more quickly in another state. Then he came to the point. He has a number of shares of stock in the Coffeepot Oil Company. He said he practically wanted to make me a present of fifty shares. I was very courteous to him and tried to restrain my real feelings."

The Doc sits up. "You are a wise man, Professor," he says. "What did Chenery mean when he said he was practically making you a present of the stock?"

"The market price on the shares is over three hundred," Speevle says. "Chenery is going to let me have them for only one hundred dollars per share. He said he needs some cash for this trip or he would give them to me outright."

The Doc frowns. "I have had wide experience with oil stocks of various kinds," he says. "Coffeepot is an excellent company. If these shares are genuine you will get a bargain." He turns to Cornelius. "The first thing is to check on the ownership of this stock. I suggest that you go into Hoedown Junction this evening and send a telegram to the company. I think you will find that the stock is listed in his name but we want to be very certain."

Cornelius swallows his drink and gets up. His freckled face is puzzled. "If this stock is bona fide, how can Chenery profit from this deal?"

The Doc smiles. "Tell me one thing. Did Chenery insist on delivery of the cash and transfer of the stock by eleven o'clock tomorrow morning?"

Speevle stares at him. "How did you know that?"

The Doc smiles. "I know what Mr. Chenery has in mind." He sobers. "You must follow my instructions carefully, Professor. Get five thousand from the bank tomorrow morning. By that time we should have an answer from the Coffeepot Company. If they confirm Chenery's ownership of the stock I will give you final instructions at ten-thirty. And we will give Mr. Chenery a big surprise."

We are gathered in the room at ten-thirty the next morning. Professor Speevle has five thousand dollars in his pocket and Cornelius has a wire from the Coffeepot outfit stating that Howland Rutherford Chenery is listed as the owner of one hundred shares of Coffeepot stock.

The Doc picks up an envelope from the desk which has Speevle's Sanatorium printed up in the corner. He hands the envelope to Speevle.

"You must do exactly as I say, Professor. One wrong move will be fatal. I can expose Mr. Chenery, but it will not be an easy matter."

Speevle nods. "Maybelle is packed and ready to go," he says. "You must not fail, Dr. Pierce." A couple of tears the size of tennis balls roll down his cheeks. "I will do anything you say. I must save my little girl."

The Doc pats him on the shoulder. "Don't worry, we will unmask this villain." He points to the envelope. "Put your five thousand in that envelope. When the deal starts you must take the money out, count it on the table, seal the envelope and drop it on the table in front of you. It is important that you seal this envelope in a casual manner."

Speevle listens carefully. "Then what do I do?"

"Then I will examine the stock Chenery is to give you. We will explain our presence by saying that you do not trust Chenery. He may squawk a little but he will go through with the deal anyhow. If I nod to you it means that the stock is the genuine article. However, do not hand Chenery the envelope containing the money until you actually have the stock in your hands. I believe the stock will also be in an envelope."

Cornelius Potts is frowning. "This sounds like a lot of nonsense. If the stock is genuine, why all this hocus-pocus with envelopes?"

The Doc smiles. "Because the hand is quicker than the eye," he says. "We will join you in the office in five minutes. There are certain arrangements I have to make in the meantime."

I CAN see that Cornelius and the professor are both thoroughly confused, and I have to admit I am in kind of a fog myself. Although I begin to get an idea when I see the Doc take another envelope from the desk after Cornelius and Speevle have gone. He stuffs this envelope with paper, seals and puts it in the side pocket of his swayback coat.

A few minutes before eleven we are sitting around the table in Speevle's office. The Doc has placed everybody the way he wants them. The professor is at the head with the Doc on his left and Cornelius on his right. I am at the other end of the table and Chenery is sitting between me and the Doc.

Of course Chenery puts up a complaint when he finds we are present, but Speevle says five thousand dollars is a large sum and he brings the Doc in as an expert on oil stock. For a minute I think Chenery is going to walk out but the professor pulls out the envelope and starts counting the money and Chenery sits tight.

The money is in hundreds and by the time the professor has counted out fifty of them my hands are itching and Chenery is practically drooling.

Speevle tucks the wad of lettuce back into the envelope, licks the flap and lays it on the table in front of him.

Chenery pulls out an envelope, a brown manila job, and hands the stock over to the Doc. "Take a good look, expert," he says. "If you find anything wrong I'll eat it."

The Doc takes a quick gander and shoves the stock back in the envelope. "These are genuine shares of Coffeepot," he says. "You are getting a great bargain, Professor."

Chenery grins. "Let's get it over with," he says. "I've got to catch a train." He raises up out of his chair to hand the envelope to the professor. As he reaches across the table his chair falls over. He turns around with a startled look on his face, then he grins again. "My nerves are not too good," he says. He slides the envelope across the table and sits down again. I have thoughtfully put his chair back in place.

The professor glances at the green certificates sticking out of the envelope and shoves them in his pocket. He watches Chenery get to his feet and there is a sad look on the old man's face. Chenery turns and starts for the door. "You will excuse my sudden departure, I'm sure," he says.

I am right behind him and when the Doc gives me the office I put the arm on Chenery and shove him back into his chair. He snarls and glares up at me. "What is this, a stick-up?"

The Doc smiles at him. "Nothing so crude," he says. "I did not want you to leave until the deal was completed." He puts his hand in Chenery's coat pocket and pulls out a brown envelope. He drops it on the table and looks at Cornelius. "Open that envelope, Mr. Potts, and compare its contents with the contents of the envelope in Professor Speevle's pocket."

Speevle's blue eyes are like saucers. He drops the envelope out of his pocket and shakes the green papers out on the table. Chenery is twisting but not too much. I am itching to clip him and he knows it.

The Doc taps one of the certificates with a finger.

"This is the genuine stock," he says. "You will notice that it is engraved. The envelope which finally wound up in Professor Speevle's pocket contains bogus stock which is printed." He taps another certificate. "You will also notice that the signatures are blurred on the bogus stock."

Cornelius comes around the table. "Let me have that scoundrel for a minute," he tells me. "I want to see how he will look with his teeth pushed in."

The Doc gets to his feet, looks hurriedly at his watch.

"I think you'll agree we have carried out our part of the bargain, gentlemen," he says. He points to the certificates on the table. "The possession of that bogus stock should place Mr. Chenery behind bars for a long period." He pats the professor on the shoulder. "With your permission we will have Herman drive us to the station. I think your daughter's opinion of Mr. Chenery will undergo a drastic revision."

The professor grips the Doc's big mitt. "I can never thank you enough, Dr. Pierce. Whatever you are, you have saved my little girl."

The Doc grins. "Don't forget that I also saved you fifty shares of Coffeepot oil stock, worth fifteen thousand dollars on the market."

WE ARE on the train before the Doc says a word. He stretches out his legs and gives me a big grin. "Quite an interesting little experience, pony boy. I look back on it with a great deal of satisfaction."

"Well," I tell him, "it has been interesting but I will be better satisfied if we make a score of some kind. We are not holding much in the way of money right now."

The Doc's grin spreads all over his big red face. He reaches in his pocket and pulls out an envelope with Speevle's Sanatorium printed up in the corner.

"Mr. Chenery is better than a green hand at the old switch game," he says. "But I was working that caper when Mr. Chenery had to change his pants every few minutes. When he created his little diversion by knocking over that chair and switched the good stock for the bogus, I absent-mindedly exchanged the envelope in my pocket for the one in front of Professor Speevle." He breaks the flap and riffles the lettuce through his fingers. "Somehow I don't think the professor will mind the departure of this trifling sum. He has received good value for his money and his daughter was saved from a fate that they tell me is worse than death."

He splits the stack and hands me half the banknotes.

I stow the money in my leather and grin back at him. "I figured you had fumbled it," I tell him. "I saw Chenery make the switch with the stock, but I swear I didn't see your hands move, even though I was watching for it."

The Doc shakes His head. "If we had been in a position to make a quick departure I could easily have switched that Coffeepot stock to my own pocket." He lets out a big sigh. "But I suppose we should count our blessings, and not be greedy."

THE DOCTOR'S PLANT

THE DOC SLIPS ME THE OFFICE
TO SIT STILL. I DO THIS WITH
PLENTY OF DOUBTS—I'M NOT
AS STUPID AS KATINKA VAN
POOTEN—AND I'M HEP THAT
THE "LITTLE BROTHER" TUXEDO
TOOMEY REFERS TO IS HIS
CONCEALED FIREARM AND THAT
TUXEDO WON'T HESITATE TO
THROW A SLUG AT ME.

I **BRING** the heap to a halt in front of the big iron gate in this stone wall that surrounds Bosky Bowers. The Doc leans out the window and hands the gate guard one of the cards Inky Malone printed up for us that same afternoon.

"I have an appointment with Mr. Schuykill Van Pooten," the Doc says.

The guard takes a gander at the card and nods. "Very good, Dr. Pierce. I will inform Mr. Van Pooten." He goes into the cubbyhole beside the gate and picks up a phone. I lean back in the seat and try to relax.

Of course I know very well that Bosky Bowers is inhabited by a lot of prominent citizens with large bankrolls. I also know that this stone wall is put up to keep the common people from peeking in at these prominent inhabitants, but I still feel nervous.

I am always nervous when we start a new caper and this stone wall and the iron gate and the gate guard remind me of things I would rather not think about right at this time. Also the fact that Tuxedo Toomey is mixed up in this enterprise does not make me feel better. Tuxedo Toomey has always been a short price in my book.

The reason the Doc and I are sitting outside this iron gate to Bosky Bowers is because Tuxedo Toomey comes into the hotel dining room the evening before. The Doc is working on his second steak when I spot Tuxedo heading toward us with a big smile stretched all over his face.

I am surprised at this as I am by no means on friendly terms with Tuxedo Toomey. In fact just a short while back I hang a left hook on Tuxedo's chin when he rings a pair of busters into a dice game I am attending.

Tuxedo is a tall party a couple of years older than me, maybe thirty. He has curly black hair and shiny white teeth and he is called Tuxedo because he always wears a boiled shirt and a monkey suit and hangs around places like the Ritz where he gives the inmates plenty of attention of one kind and another, especially the dames.

Tuxedo sticks out his hand. "Let us hide the hatchet, Brother Allan," he says. "Let us forget the unpleasant past and move forward in harmony to a bright and profitable future. I have a little business proposition which I am sure will be of interest to you and your partner."

I give Tuxedo a cold look and grip his mitt. "We can always use a fresh dollar," I tell him. "What's the caper?"

Tuxedo stretches his smile another notch. "You'll get the details in a moment." He turns to the Doc. "This is a most fortunate meeting, Dr. Pierce. My partner, Wall-Street Walter, claims that you are the smartest operator around."

THE DOC knows that Tuxedo is strictly short change but he likes this spiel. He sticks his thumbs in the armholes of his swayback coat and sucks up his haybelly until I think he is going to pop all the buttons off his white vest.

"Wall-Street Walter is a dear old friend," he says to Tuxedo. "I am gratified to hear of his kind remarks,

Tuxedo Toomey has his hand in his coat pocket and he
looks at me as he says: "I have Little Brother at my side,
Allan. You are too smart to pick on Little Brother."

although I suspect he has exaggerated my modest talent.
Is Walter connected with this little business proposition
you mentioned?"

Tuxedo shakes his head. "Not now," he says. "Poor old
Walter had a little difficulty with the Parole Board. The
Law has placed Walter back in college to finish out his
term."

The Doc's big red face is sad. "I regret to hear of Walter's
ill fortune." He waves at a chair. "Sit down."

Tuxedo parks it and leans across the table. "Walter's
absence has placed me in an awkward position, Dr. Pierce,"
he says. "We have this deal all readied up for the payoff.

I made the initial pitch and of course cannot handle the payoff. I hope that you and my old friend, Brother Allan, will help me out."

The Doc slips me a quick look. "Do you think we can spare the time, pony boy?"

"I don't think so," I tell him. "We have this large and important transaction on at the moment." I have a hard time keeping a straight face when I say this. The only transaction we have on is with the hotel manager. We are in the stakes for a month's rent and this manager is getting hard to handle. In fact it takes the Doc a good hour to talk this manager out of putting a hickey in our keyhole that very evening.

Tuxedo Toomey lowers his voice. "You must help me out," he says. "This trick can be turned in a couple of days and will cash out for three thousand. I collected six hundred when I made the opening pitch. We will split the remainder, twenty-four C's, down the middle."

The Doc's eyes narrow. "If we take on your proposition we split the whole take three ways. One thousand dollars each."

Tuxedo scowls, then shrugs. "I have no choice," he says. "I must accept your terms." He puts his elbows on the table. "I am going to tell you the whole story. I think it is important that you know the whole background."

"It is most important," the Doc says.

Tuxedo gives him a quick look, then goes on: "A week ago I met a young man named Fenwick Griggs in Cool-Off Flanagan's poker parlor. The cards went badly for Fenwick. He became despondent. In fact Fenwick went so far as to take several drinks of Cool-Off's house whiskey in an effort to ease his misery."

The Doc shudders. "As a medical man I do not advise consumption of the Flanagan beverage in large quantities."

I get a snicker out of this remark. The Doc's only claim to a medical handle is because he used to peddle snake-oil around the carnivals some years back—although I have to admit that when it comes to whiskey he is better than a fair judge.

Tuxedo smiles briefly. "Fortunately I managed to get Fenwick Griggs out into the air before he had taken a lethal dose. I had a flask of brandy in my pocket and gave him a quick snort as an antidote. Fenwick Griggs was grateful. In fact he insisted that I accompany him to his home in Bosky Bowers and become his guest for the night."

The Doc is now paying close attention. "Bosky Bowers," he says in a soft voice. "Then Fenwick Griggs is well-heeled?"

"According to ordinary standards, yes," Tuxedo says. "I spent a long evening in his Bosky Bowers home listening to Fenwick Griggs. Among other things, he told me that he had inherited his home and a sizable sum besides. But Fenwick likes plenty of action at the gaming tables and his fortune is now whittled down to what he regards as the ragged edge of poverty."

The Doc frowns. "Then you do not intend to make this score off Fenwick Griggs?"

Tuxedo nods. "That's right. But during this long evening, Fenwick gave me the lead to the party who is now set up for the score. This party is a crusty old widower named Schuykill Van Pooten. Schuykill is Fenwick's next-door neighbor and is also the sole parent of an attractive daughter named Katinka. Schuykill has a large bankroll and Katinka is his only heir. Fenwick has put in considerable work on Katinka and plans to mend his shattered fortunes by teaming up with her."

Well, I don't make any sense out of this long story. I slide down in my chair. "Wake me up when you get to the payoff," I tell Tuxedo. "I am weary. I spent a hot afternoon at Belmont Park trying to shoo in a couple of longshots."

TUXEDO SHOWS his teeth in a wide smile. "I am sorry if I bore you," he says. "Here is the payoff: Schuykill Van Pooten is now engaged in a one-man battle with the other residents of Bosky Bowers. The property owners in Bosky Bowers have banded together and formed a company to supply the settlement with electricity, gas and water. Schuykill Van Pooten claims the company has overcharged him. He has refused to pay his bills for two months. His services have been shut off by the company. When Fenwick Griggs told me about this I realized that Schuykill Van Pooten was an excellent prospect for the Midget Marvel Trust Buster. I, incidentally, am the sole owner of the Midget Marvel Trust Buster."

I sit up straight in my chair but before I can say anything the Doc lets out a pleased chuckle.

"I gather that this Midget Marvel is a small power plant, built for use in private homes," he announces.

"You have an alert mind, Dr. Pierce," Tuxedo says. "According to the descriptive literature printed in three colors on glossy paper, the Midget Marvel will provide all the power necessary to run the average household at a cost far below the exorbitant rates charged by public utility companies. That is why it is called the Trust Buster."

The Doc lets out another chuckle. "A clever pitch," he says. "I assume that this Midget Marvel Trust Buster exists only in the pages of this descriptive literature."

THE DOCTOR'S PLANT 219

"Right again," Tuxedo tells him. "About a year ago, when I first became interested in the Midget Marvel, the inventor constructed a full-scale model for the purpose of accelerating the sale of stock. The first time the Midget Marvel was placed in operation the motor exploded and damaged the inventor to such an extent that he was placed in a room with padded walls. That was how I obtained control of this invention. Since that unfortunate occurrence I have felt it prudent to confine the Midget Marvel to the pages of the booklet."

"Very wise," the Doc says. He leans back and stares at the ceiling. "I believe I have the general idea," he says finally. "What leadoff did you use on this old guy, Schuykill Van Pooten?"

"The old half-price-contract gag," Tuxedo tells him. "I made the initial pitch as a salesman named J.H. Simpson. Wall-Street Walter was scheduled to give him the ground-floor-stock follow-up."

The Doc hauls out his cheaters with the black ribbon and places them on his nose. He takes out his notebook. "J.H. Simpson," he says. "I must make notes of these details." He looks at Tuxedo. "You are a smart boy. What is your general impression of Schuykill Van Pooten?"

"A Mary Pickford," Tuxedo tells him. "A sweetheart, a natural score. Schuykill got all his pelf from his old man. He has never made a dollar under his own power in his life. So of course Schuykill regards himself as a shrewd businessman."

The Doc nods. "It has been my good fortune to meet many such during my career. I shall look forward to meeting Schuykill Van Pooten not later than tomorrow night." He gets to his feet. "You must excuse us now, Mr. Toomey."

He shoots me a quick look. "We will have to lay our plans carefully, pony boy."

The next morning we go down to Inky Malone's shop. He does a quick printing job for us. The Doc calls Schuykill Van Pooten on the phone and makes a date. So now we are here at the gate of Bosky Bowers.

The guard finally comes out of his cubbyhole and opens the gate. He points up the gravel drive. "Mr. Van Pooten lives in the fourth house on the right."

Once this stone wall is behind us I find out that Bosky Bowers is a pleasant place, at that. The houses are big and have plenty of lawns and flowers around them. It is just getting dark but most of the windows are blazing with light. All but the fourth house on the right.

Schuykill Van Pooten's residence is dark, except for a weak glow in one downstairs window.

The Doc elbows me and chuckles softly. "I have a feeling Schuykill will be easy to fineprint under the primitive illumination he is using."

I grin back at him. I am not so nervous now. I halt the heap in front of the porch and follow the Doc up the steps. Before I can punch the bell the door opens and a party in a white jacket appears. I give this party a quick run-down and I am suddenly nervous again.

This party is about the Doc's age, maybe fifty, but he has shoulders on him like a buffalo. He is easily six-feet-four-inches tall and has a big chin. His voice sounds like it comes up out of a tunnel.

"Dr. Pierce?" he rumbles. The Doc nods and hands his black skimmer to this buffalo. I trust him with my hat and we follow him down a wide hall that is lighted by a candle on a table at the far end. The buffalo knocks at a door and opens it.

SCHUYKILL VAN POOTEN is sitting behind a shiny desk in a room with books lining the walls. The light of a pair of tall candles is flickering on his bald head. He has a fat, round face and a pair of blue eyes you could use to bore holes in a brick wall.

The Doc puts me away as his confidential secretary and we sit down. The way the Doc starts out I realize he is going to make this a quick pitch.

"I'll be brief, Mr. Van Pooten," he says. "You have been the victim of a clever swindle. I am here to rectify that if it is possible."

Schuykill Van Pooten's eyes bug out and he hops about three feet in the air. "Swindle!" he yells. "What swindle?"

The Doc lifts a hand. "Please be calm," he says. "I am referring to the man you knew as J.H. Simpson. I regret to inform you that J.H. Simpson is not connected with my company."

Schuykill is very lively on the next hop. "What's that? Simpson not connected with the company?"

He reaches into the desk drawer and throws a green paper at the Doc. "There's the contract. Right down in black and white."

The Doc shakes his head and looks sad. "This is most unfortunate," he says. He puts the green paper back on the desk without looking at it. "From a strictly legal standpoint my company is not bound by any contract entered into by an unauthorized person such as Simpson. On the other hand we realize that you have suffered a grave injustice. I am here to discuss the terms of a possible settlement with you."

Schuykill Van Pooten hollers so loud it bounces off the ceiling. "Terms," he yells. "Settlement! I gave that scoundrel Simpson six hundred dollars! He promised to install a power plant in my home for half-price—fifteen hundred dollars!"

The Doc's red face gets even sadder. "Even if Simpson had been connected with my company, the board of directors would never accept such a contract. We have set the police on Simpson's trail but he has fled the country, taking your six hundred dollars and his other ill-gotten gains with him."

Van Pooten sits there with his mouth open while this sinks in. Before he can say anything the door opens and a young filly bounces into the room. I figure this is Katinka, the sole heir of Schuykill Van Pooten so I take a good gander at her. She has blond hair and rosy cheeks and right now she is not hard to take, although it is a cinch she will pack plenty of weight for her age in a few years.

"What is wrong, Daddy?" she asks. She frowns at the Doc. "Please do not upset my father. His heart is not strong."

The Doc puts on a big smile and gets to his feet. I get up, too. The Doc says: "We are here to help your father, Miss Van Pooten. I have just informed him that he has been the victim of a clever swindler. Naturally he is upset."

Schuykill Van Pooten starts to work up another holler but the dame puts a hand over his mouth.

"Hush, Daddy," she tells him. She smiles at the Doc. "I trust you, sir. You have a kind and honest face."

Well, I am not surprised to hear her say this. The Doc has been peddling his kind and honest face for a good many years. He bows at the dame. "Thank you, my dear. I am Dr. Pierce and this is my friend and secretary, Mr. Allan."

The dame gives me a quick look and sits down in the chair the Doc pulls up for her. "What is this all about?"

The Doc turns to Schuykill Van Pooten. "Exactly what was the deal J.H. Simpson offered you?"

Van Pooten works his chin up and down like he is chewing a sour cud. "Half-price," he says. "Simpson said the regular price for this power plant was three thousand. He said if I gave him the regular down payment of six hundred dollars he'd make out the contract for an additional nine hundred and guarantee that it would be installed in a week. Simpson said the company wanted customers like me."

The Doc nods. "On that one point Simpson was right," he says. "We are anxious to have satisfied customers of your social and financial standing on our list. But I am afraid that the board of directors will not honor this contract. Not as it stands now."

Schuykill Van Pooten sits up in his chair and snaps at the bait. "Do you mean there is some way you can honor this contract?"

The Doc smiles. "Of course. That is why I came here tonight. Frankly," he says, "I would like to number you among our customers. A man of your prestige, business acumen and independent mind would be of great value to the company in our struggle against the forces of financial oppression as represented by the power trust."

The light from the pair of candles is shaky and dim but I can see this look come into Schuykill Van Pooten's little blue eyes. The same look I have seen a hundred times. He figures he is about to cash in on his high opinion of himself. He is hooked—but good.

JUST THEN there is a knock at the door. The door swings open and this buffalo in the white jacket is standing there. Van Pooten snaps: "What is it, Cowgill?"

Cowgill's voice comes up out of the tunnel. "Mr. Fenwick Griggs, the gentleman who lives next door, is here to see Miss Katinka. He says it is very important that he see her immediately."

Van Pooten snorts but Katinka lays a hand over his mouth. "I'll be right back, Daddy," she says. She smiles at the Doc. "I hope you will excuse me." The Doc nods and we watch her swish out the door. The Doc has a little grin on his face.

He turns to Schuykill Van Pooten. "You asked if there was some way we could honor this contract. My answer is yes. Our stockholders are given the privilege of buying a power plant for their own homes at half-price. I am sure that under the circumstances the board of directors will be willing to waive the six-hundred-dollar down payment and charge it off to profit and loss. A small purchase of stock in this vigorous and virile company will not only entitle you to this privilege but will return a tidy profit on your investment."

Schuykill Van Pooten screws up his face in a smile. He is being shrewd again. "How much stock must I buy?"

The Doc is thinking fast, trying to decide how much of a score Van Pooten will hold still for. I am getting nervous again. When the door opens I jump a foot. Katinka comes into the room and she is not smiling now. She points her finger at the Doc and her plump red lips are trembling.

"This man is an impostor, Daddy," she says. "He is here for no good purpose. Mr. Griggs came over especially to warn us."

I figure it is time to go. I get to my feet but the Doc slips me the office to sit still. He still has this little grin on his face. "That is a strong statement, Miss Van Pooten," he says. "I believe I am entitled to an explanation."

Katinka sniffs and speaks to her father. "I know you do not approve of Fenwick Griggs, Daddy," she says, "but he has just rendered us a real service. He saw these men come in and he recognized them as shady characters."

Schuykill Van Pooten snorts. "That young whippersnapper! I wouldn't trust him around the corner."

Katinka's round face is pink. "Then I'll let him tell you himself." She raises her voice. "Please come in, Fenwick."

Tuxedo Toomey walks into the room.

I sit still in my chair for two reasons. One is that this buffalo butler, Cowgill, is standing in the doorway with a mean look on his big face. The other is because Tuxedo Toomey has his right hand in his coat pocket and the first words he says are aimed right at me.

"I have Little Brother at my side, Brother Allan, he says. "You are too smart to pick on Little Brother."

Well, of course I know that when Tuxedo speaks of Little Brother he is referring to a firearm he has concealed in his coat pocket but Katinka is puzzled. She looks up at Tuxedo.

"What a strange thing to say, Fenwick. What do you mean?"

Tuxedo skips the question and turns to Schuykill Van Pooten. "I am just being a good neighbor," he says. "A detective friend pointed these men out to me some weeks ago. He said they are well-known confidence men although the police have never been able to get enough evidence to convict them. He said their latest swindle was the sale of stock in a phony power plant called the Midget Marvel Trust Buster."

Schuykill Van Pooten slaps his hand on the desk and grabs the telephone. "I'll give the police evidence," he yells. "One of their confederates got six hundred dollars of my money." He glares at the Doc. "So your stockholders get the privilege of buying at half price!"

WELL, IT'S coming pretty fast. It takes me some time to get used to the idea that Tuxedo Toomey is living in Bosky Bowers under the name of Fenwick Griggs. I am beginning to understand why Tuxedo tells us this long tale about Fenwick Griggs but I don't have time to put it all together right then. I am watching this big butler, Cowgill, and figuring the odds. They don't add up. Tuxedo Toomey has Little Brother in his coat pocket and I know now that he will not hesitate to throw a slug at me. I also realize that Tuxedo remembers that punch I laid on his chin during the dice game.

The Doc leans back in his chair and lets out a chuckle. "This is ridiculous," he says. He looks at Tuxedo Toomey. "Are you sure that you want Mr. Van Pooten to call the police? It might prove embarrassing to you, Mr. Fenwick Griggs."

Tuxedo looks worried all of a sudden. He reaches across the desk and takes the phone out of Schuykill Van Pooten's hand.

"On second thought," he says, "I think it would be unwise to call the police. If these men go to jail you will still be out your six hundred dollars. I have a better idea. I suggest that if these two crooks agree to refund your six hundred dollars, we agree to let them go. It might be difficult to get them convicted on the evidence we have."

The Doc's big red face is suddenly hard. "What evidence?" He reaches over and picks the sales contract off the desk. He puts on his cheaters and looks at this green document closely. "It may interest you gentlemen to know that I have never heard of the Midget Marvel Trust

Buster," he says slowly. "I am a major stockholder in the Farmer's Friendly Favorite, a sound company, listed on the Stock Exchange."

Well, Tuxedo Toomey is a smart operator and nobody can deny that he has plenty of moxie. But when the Doc springs this line, Tuxedo turns white as a sheet. His grip tightens on Little Brother in his pocket and his voice shakes.

"That is a lie, Pierce," he tells the Doc. "At this very moment you have a bundle of Midget Marvel shares in your pocket."

The Doc chuckles again, reaches into his pocket and lays a sheaf of pink papers on the desk. "Take a look at these, Mr. Van Pooten," he says. "You will find they are shares in the Farmer's Friendly Favorite Company."

Schuykill Van Pooten has been moving his head back and forth between the Doc and Tuxedo like he is watching a ping-pong game. He moves one of the candles closer, squints his eyes and takes a close gander at the papers the Doc lays on the desk. He looks up at Tuxedo Toomey. "I have never trusted you, young man," he says. "These shares of stock are exactly what Dr. Pierce says they are—shares in the Farmer's Friendly Favorite Company."

The Doc grins at Tuxedo who is now two shades whiter. "No apology is necessary, Mr. Fenwick Griggs," he says. "But I think a few questions are in order." He turns to Katinka. "How long has this man who calls himself Fenwick Griggs been a neighbor of yours?"

Katinka looks at Tuxedo but he is now staring at the floor although he still keeps his hand on Little Brother in his pocket. "He rented the house next door about two months ago," she says.

"I thought so," the Doc tells her. He turns to Schuykill Van Pooten. "This J.H. Simpson who collected six hundred dollars from you, what did he look like?"

Van Pooten thinks for a minute. "About fifty," he says. "Short, thick-set, ruddy face, very smooth talker."

The Doc glances at me. "Wall-Street Walter," he says in a soft voice. "Just as I suspected." He looks at Schuykill Van Pooten. "You have a keen, analytical mind," he says. "You realize now that the man you know as Fenwick Griggs is an adventurer. His chief interest in your household is your lovely daughter." He leans forward and jabs a finger at Tuxedo Toomey. "Can you deny this? You came here tonight in a brazen effort to cast a stigma upon me, an honest businessman, in the hope that you could ingratiate yourself with Mr. Van Pooten. I challenge you, Mr. Fenwick Griggs!" He reaches for the telephone. "Shall we call the police and match records? Shall we let the police decide who is the honest man and who is the crook?"

WELL, IN all the years I have teamed with the Doc I never see him put on a better performance. Of course we always operate strictly on the side of the law, or just this side of it. And I know Tuxedo has been tagged for a couple of short stretches in the pen. But even at that it makes me nervous when the Doc speaks of calling the cops.

Schuykill Van Pooten taps his fingers on the desk and gives Tuxedo a cold look. "How about it, Griggs?"

Tuxedo knows when he has over-matched himself. He turns toward the door. "Very well," he says. "If you prefer the word of a known criminal against that of an honest neighbor, I leave you to your fate."

Van Pooten wiggles a finger at this buffalo butler in the doorway. "Take him out, Cowgill," he says, very crisp. Cowgill grips Tuxedo Toomey by the slack in his pants.

As Tuxedo goes by I reach out and snag Little Brother out of his coat pocket. Little Brother is a Colt .38 and when I have this roscoe in my own coat pocket I do not feel so nervous, although I never fired off a gun in my life.

There is a thumping and bumping in the hallway. In a minute Cowgill comes back with a pleased look on his face. "Mr. Fenwick Griggs is out, sir," he says.

Van Pooten gives him a tight smile. "Good," he says. "You may go now, Cowgill."

Katinka is on her feet and her pink face is sad. She follows the butler out the door without saying a word. I can understand how she feels. Tuxedo Toomey is a good-looking young buck, at that.

The Doc picks up the sheaf of pink papers from the desk. "We will take our departure, Mr. Van Pooten," he says. "At some future date I would like to discuss the advantages of the Farmer's Friendly Favorite with you, but I know that you are not interested at this time."

Schuykill Van Pooten grins. He reaches into a drawer in the desk and places a bottle and three glasses on the top. "You must not leave now, Dr. Pierce," he says. "You have done me a service. I knew that my daughter was interested in Fenwick Griggs. You have shown him to be the sort of man no woman can trust." He looks at me. "Will you close the door, Mr. Allan? If Cowgill or my daughter suspected the existence of this bottle they would take it away from me and my doctor would scold me."

I am still nervous but when the Doc gives me the office I get up and shut the door. Van Pooten pours a big dose in each glass and leans back in his chair. "I have not had such a lively evening in years," he says. "You must tell me the whole story. I know you have been holding something back."

The Doc takes a big swallow from his glass. "Your astute mind has penetrated to the heart of this situation, Mr. Van Pooten," he says. "Mr. Allan here is Chief Investigator for our company. He learned that a man named J.H. Simpson was making fake sales of a private power plant called the Midget Marvel Trust Buster. Mr. Allan tracked this fake concern to its source. The man behind the Midget Marvel was the man you knew as Fenwick Griggs."

Van Pooten has swallowed his first dose of bourbon and it is beginning to take hold. "Always knew that Griggs was a scoundrel," he says.

The Doc moves in fast. "As the largest company in the field of home power plants, we were naturally interested in the activities of the Midget Marvel Trust Buster backers. The sale of fake plants and fake stock reflects on our whole industry."

Van Pooten now is on his second dose of bourbon. He nods his head. "Reflects on the whole industry," he says.

The Doc slips me a wink. "This man you knew as Fenwick Griggs is well-known to the police under the name of Toomey. He was directly responsible for stirring up the trouble between you and the other residents of Bosky Bowers. He also employed his masculine charms in an attempt to form a marital alliance with your daughter. He is a deep-dyed villain, a bigamist, and the father of six starving children."

SCHUYKILL VAN POOTEN'S glass is empty again so I give him another charge. He bobs his head at me and reaches across the desk. He grips the Doc by the mitt. "You are my friend," he says. "You saved my little girl from the clutches of a scoundrel."

The Doc picks up the sheaf of pink papers. "My only regret is that we cannot have the benefit of your business sagacity in the conduct of the business of the Farmer's Friendly Favorite Company." He picks up his glass. "We will have one more drink with you and then Mr. Allan and I will leave."

Schuykill Van Pooten dumps the next dose of bourbon down his throat. "Half-price," he says. He reaches in the desk and pulls out a checkbook. "Want to be a stockholder. Got to have power plant. How much?"

The Doc shuffles the stack of pink papers. "Four thousand dollars will put you on our board of directors, and will also place a Farmer's Friendly Favorite power plant in your home within a week."

Van Pooten scribbles in the checkbook. "Business sagacity," he says. "Half-price."

The next morning we are waiting on the doormat when the bank opens. As we walk down the street I can feel the comfort of two grand against my chest. I look up at the Doc. "Look," I tell him, "I can figure most of this deal. But how did you know that Tuxedo Toomey was passing himself off as Fenwick Griggs out in Bosky Bowers, and how did you happen to have this Farmer's Friendly Favorite stock on you?"

The Doc chuckles. "I knew that Tuxedo Toomey was not fond of you. Also the story about the mythical Fenwick Griggs was too long and too detailed. Schuykill Van Pooten was the payoff and there was no reason for bringing Fenwick Griggs into the story at all. Another tip-off was when Tuxedo Toomey agreed to a three-way payoff. I suspected that Tuxedo had something to do with Wall

Street Walter's sudden return to the pen. Tuxedo tried to use us as a means of setting himself in with Schuykill Van Pooten and Katinka. He also tried to pay you off for poking him in the jaw. I had the Farmer's Friendly Favorite stock on me because I talked Inky Malone into staking me to one share of it. Yesterday morning he printed up the rest of the shares Schuykill Van Pooten now possesses, using the share I bought as a model."

"Well," I tell the Doc, "I have to admit that Tuxedo had me going on this Midget Marvel deal. But now that we are back in the chips and can pay our way out of the hotel stakes I have a different plant in mind. I intend to plant a left hook on this hotel manager's chin before we check out."

The Doc chuckles. "That is one plant that has my hearty approval."